By Henry Daniel Archunde Jr

Six Minutes Late

It Doesn't Rain Forever

The Letter He Never Sent

The Letter He Never Sent
By
Henry Daniel Archunde Jr

True North Writings

Arizona

Published by True North Writings
Edited By: *Ana Archunde*
ISBN: 979-8-9934077-8-4
Library of Congress Control Number: 2026908125

Book Design by Mr. & Mrs. Archunde

Dedication
For my daughters,
whose light reminds me that love never stops reaching.
Even when the years and miles try to stand in its way.
Every word on these pages is a door left open for you.

A Father's Promise
I may not have held your hand each dawn,
nor heard your laughter fill the years,
but I have carried you in every season.
Through silence, through ache, through hope.
One day, when time grows kind again,
You will see I never stopped writing to you.
And in the ink between these lines, you will find the part of me that never let
go.

• Henry Daniel Archunde Jr.

Table of Contents

The Letter He Never Sent

Prologue ~ The Taking

The night smelled of rain and rust when they took Eleanor away. Sierra Mesa, Arizona, was caught between seasons that day. The kind of winter evening when the desert forgot its own heat and the clouds pressed low, thick with their rare promise. Rain gathered in the gutters. It slicked the courthouse steps and traced slow lines through the dust that never truly washed off its stone.

Miles Bennett stood at the bottom of those steps, rain sliding down his neck, watching the red dress vanish into the blur of headlights. The woman wearing it, Lydia Harper, moved with the extraordinary precision of someone who had already decided what the world owed her. Her lipstick matched the dress, painted red like warning signs and stoplights, the kind of color that made surrender look deliberate. When she buckled Eleanor into the car seat, she did not look back. Not at him.

Not at the man who had whispered only loving things to that child every night of her eight months on earth, humming old lullabies off-key until her fists unclenched and sleep found her. The car door closed with a sound like the end of something. Then the engine turned. The tires hissed on the wet street, and Miles was left standing there with nothing but his own reflection rippling in the puddles.

Inside the courthouse, the echo of the gavel still rang in his ears. The judge's voice, measured, distant, had pronounced what felt like a sentence, though no crime had been named. "You lack stability, Mr. Bennett. Love, while admirable, is not a legal foundation." Miles had nothing to give the judge but words, and words are soft currency when the world demands proof.

He had said, "I love her," and the law had replied, "Do you have a lease in your name?" Do you have pay stubs? A refrigerator with food?" He had told the truth. That the roof above him was borrowed, that hunger had left its gray thumbprint on too many days, that he was trying to become the kind of man who could hold a life steady. The gavel found the wood, a sound too small for what it ended. Lydia's lawyer gathered his papers with practiced calm, his eyes already elsewhere, on the following case, the following story that was not this one.

Across the aisle, Miles sat as if the air itself had turned solid, the silence heavy enough to bruise. Somewhere down the hall, a clerk laughed at a joke that would survive the afternoon. Proof that the world, indifferent and tireless, was already moving on. But Miles was not. Not yet. He stayed long after the room emptied, his hands clasped so tightly his knuckles ached. His heart was shaped like a house, with every door locked. When he finally stepped outside, the rain had grown meaner. It fell sideways under the courthouse lights, sharp as pins.

Miles walked with his head down, his breath ghosting in the cold, his thoughts spilling backward through every choice that had led him here. He had no umbrella. His shoes were soaked through the toes. Every few blocks, a car passed and splashed water over his cuff, but he barely noticed. His mind was somewhere else, with the child in the yellow dress, the one whose hair smelled faintly of milk and morning.

In his pocket, he felt for the ribbon, pale yellow, frayed at one edge, still sweet with the powdery scent of Eleanor's drawer. He had tied it around her wrist once, when she was only weeks old, pretending it was a bracelet. She had waved it like sunlight.

He walked past shuttered storefronts and a diner
still open; the neon sign flickering EAT in halfhearted
persistence. A man inside mopped the floor, humming a
tune Miles almost recognized. When he reached his small
apartment, one room above the laundromat, he did not
bother with the lights. The hum of the machines below
rattled through the floor, familiar and grounding. He hung
his coat on a nail, placed the ribbon on the windowsill, and
stood for a moment watching the rain collect on the glass.

The city shimmered under the storm. The streetlights
burned in puddles like miniature, drowned suns. Somewhere
nearby, thunder grumbled across the valley, and the sound
rolled through his chest like grief learning how to breathe.
Miles sat on the mattress, the only furniture he owned
besides a table and a chair and tried to memorize what
remained. The slope of Eleanor's cheek against his chest,
the way her fingers curled around his shirt as though fabric
could be an anchor against the tide.

Lydia's red, he thought, was the color of stop signs, of
sirens, of every door closing. Around him lay the colors
that would follow for years: the brown of secondhand
furniture, the gray of winter windows, the watered blue
of cheap dish soap that never quite cut the grease. Still,
when the lamp warmed the room to its small gold, he could
believe in a softer world. He could believe in candles and
birthdays, in promises made to an empty seat at the table.

That night, he began a habit that became a kind of prayer.
Miles found a half-used composition notebook. One that
had once held grocery lists, phone numbers, reminders of
a different kind of life, and opened it to a clean page. The
apartment was too quiet. The clock clicked like distant
footsteps.

The scent of Eleanor's baby blanket lingered on the back of his chair. He could not bring himself to move it.

He pressed the pen down, and the words came out trembling but true.

✳ ⌐ ✳

My little star,

Tonight, I heard the sky crying and thought it was you. I know it is not. You are held. You are fed. You are sleeping.

Your breath is small and brave, unaware that the world has already made choices for us both.

They told me I am not enough. I am not yet.

But I am your father, and if there is any strength in me at all, I will spend it loving you, even if all I have left are these letters, written to the space where you should be.

✳ ⌐ ✳

Miles set the pen down and stared at the ink until it blurred. Somewhere outside, a train passed. A sound like distance made real, and for the first time since the gavel fell, Miles Bennett let himself cry. He dated the page. Tore it out carefully, folded it into quarters, and slid it into a shoe box he'd kept from a pair of boots he'd once bought on clearance. The kind meant to last a season, but he'd worn them through three, until the soles peeled like tired lips and the leather learned the shape of his days.

The box still smelled faintly of dust and rubber, of long hours and longer roads. He placed it beside his mattress as though setting down something sacred. The sound the cardboard paper made was slight, but in that silence, it might as well have been thunder. Then he wrote another page. And another. He wrote until the words began to blur, until his hand cramped and the pen left smudges across his fingertips. He wrote until the rain softened, until it stopped trying to punish the earth and instead began to soothe it.

14

★ ✿ ★

Outside, Sierra Mesa glowed faintly, neon from the diner shimmering in puddles like restless ghosts. Somewhere, a freight train moaned across the valley, its whistle carrying through the rain like a lost prayer. Inside, the single lamp hummed. The clock on the counter ticked too loudly, measuring not time but distance. Miles leaned his head back against the wall, his eyes burning from the effort of staying awake. The pages lay scattered across the floor like fallen leaves. Each one a small piece of him, written to someone who could not yet read.

When at last the pen slipped from his fingers, the rain had thinned to mist. The city's neon lights spilled through the blinds and turned the walls into a patchwork of trembling colors of pink, blue, and the weak white of the streetlamp outside. He closed his eyes, the smell of wet pavement and ink thick in the room. His last thought before sleep took him was simple, half-formed, but certain. If love cannot reach her yet, words will. And with that, he drifted off.

His body curled toward the shoe box, his breath rising and falling with the rhythm of a man dreaming of doors that never latched. In the morning, sunlight cut through the blinds, laying thin stripes across the floor. The world smelled of damp asphalt and laundromat soap. Miles pressed the yellow ribbon between two pages of *Great Expectations*, its spine cracked and smelling faintly of dust and someone else's dreams and went to look for work.

The judge had been right about the bed, the food, the pay stubs. Love did not balance a checkbook. Love did not fill a refrigerator or provide a home. But love, stubborn and wordless, could still make a man rise when exhaustion pressed hard.

Love could steady a trembling hand on the wheel, even when the road ahead refused to promise anything. Miles found day labor where he could in warehouses, loading docks, and small jobs that asked for his back more than his name. Each paycheck was a note of apology folded inside hope he could not yet send. At night, he wrote. When words failed him, he simply dated the page; proof that he had survived another day for her. Years would happen.

He did not know that yet. He only knew this was the beginning: the door was closed for now, and he kept his hand against it anyway, feeling for the hinge, trusting it might one day move beneath his touch. That night, he whispered the first of eighteen birthdays into the quiet. *"Happy birthday, my little star,"* he said, though the day was not yet hers.

He said it to learn the shape of the words. To feel them form against emptiness, to make them real before the world could take them away. He promised himself he would still be here when they finally belonged, when Eleanor could hear them from him and know they had been waiting. The candlelight flickered across the kitchen's chipped tile.

The room was small, but he had cleared a place for this ritual. One plate, one ribbon, one moment of belief. The air smelled faintly of coffee and rain that had not yet fallen. Outside, the clouds thinned to a worn blue, and through the narrow slice of alley, a patch of sky appeared, tired, but open. Miles stared at it as if it could hear him think. Hold fast, he told himself. Build a life. Keep the door open. He imagined her somewhere warm; a crib beneath a window, the sound of a lullaby he had never heard.

And as he watched that small square of sky, he thought, not aloud, but deep enough for heaven to hear.

I am yours, Eleanor, even across the miles between our names.

Empty Cradle

In the year that followed, the seasons taught him their colors again. Winter first, gray upon gray. Steam lifted from maintenance holes like something lost, learning how to leave. Miles worked wherever hands were needed. He stocked shelves in the hours when the grocery store belonged to radio songs and humming fluorescent lights. He hauled scrap from basements where the air tasted like cold pennies. He swept out a warehouse whose owner would never learn his name.

On his breaks, he would stand outside with his coffee and watch the sky lighten along the edges. That thin suggestion of gold arrived each morning no matter who had won the day before. Not long after, Miles learned the price of things. A bus ride to the South Side cost the last coins from a jar. A week of rice and beans cost the day's calluses. A secondhand crib cost him a kind stranger and a hard swallow. He tucked the receipt with the letters as if proof of loss could become proof of love.

The pastor gave him odd-hour cleaning shifts from a budget that had no room. "You'll pay me back," the man said softly. The apartment shed its shame slowly. He sanded a thrift-store table until the wood rose warm beneath his hands. He bought two plates and one bowl, though there was no child to spill cereal or argue over spoons. The plates did not match.

One white, one the shade of rain. He liked the imperfection. It suggested that someday, someone might notice. Miles set them on the thrifted table and stood there longer than the moment required, palms resting on the wood as if blessing it. He let himself be a man who believed in breakfast. Not for what it fed, but for what it meant.

The world had turned. The night had passed. Something
ordinary could still begin again. At the grocery store, he
would slow near the aisle that hurt the most. The one with
tiny clothes, pacifiers, soft spoons, and bright packages of
wonders The shelves looked like they were holding hope
for sale in pastel. Blue and pink, he thought, were the colors
of arguments, of the world's insistence on sorting love into
teams. But yellow, yellow was a mercy, a small rebellion.

Yellow said: Not yet decided, not divided. Miles reached
out once, ran his thumb along a package of socks no bigger
than a matchbox car. The cotton was soft, ribbed like
memory. He did not buy them, he had learned the cruel
arithmetic of hope, but he held them long enough for the
warmth of his hand to leave something behind. A mother
passed, pushing a cart that held a child still new enough to
marvel at ceiling lights.

The baby's gaze met him for half a second; a blink of
shared wonder before the cart rolled on. He exhaled slowly,
the air trembling out of him like something released from
a long-held note. He told himself he had come for bread
and Sun Vista beans, nothing more. Still, when he left, he
carried an invisible thing heavier than groceries.

The shape of what a future might have been, folded
small and stored somewhere under the ribs. That night,
he placed the receipt in his envelope marked proof. Not
because it proved anything, but because it belonged with
the others: tiny evidence of trying.

Then he sat at the table, poured coffee, and wrote another
letter.

✳ ⚷ ✳

My little star,
Today I touched a pair of socks small enough to rest in
my palm.

I did not buy them, but I carried them all the way home in thought. That is what love is, the ache you do not spend but cannot put down.

I kept imagining you waking one morning with one sock missing, your tiny foot bare and brave, and me searching for the other; finding it caught in your blanket, or tucked between the bars of your bassinet, a trace of warmth still waiting to be seen.

✳ ⛌ ✳

The first birthday came with a cake he did not eat.

Miles set one candle in the middle and lit it, then sat with his elbows on the scratched table and told stories to the air. He told the story of the day Eleanor was born, how the light in the hospital had been yellow and kind, how the nurse had tucked the baby into the crook of his arm, and how the baby had made that soft new-creature sound, like language without vowels.

He told the story of rain, courtrooms, and ribbons. He told the story of the room they were in, small but honest, with a plant he was trying not to kill. When the candle guttered, he did not blow it out. He cupped his hand around it and waited until the flame found its own way into smoke.

Later, Miles wrote again.

✳ ⛌ ✳

My little star,

Today I made a cake. A small one, the kind that comes from a box, though I whisked it slowly enough to feel like it mattered. I can almost hear you laughing at me; that soft, surprised laugh that lives somewhere between joy and disbelief. The thought of it fills the kitchen like sunlight, warming even the quiet corners.

20

The cake sank a little in the middle, like it forgot how to hold itself up. The frosting turned out uneven, a rough sea of sugar and hope.

Still, I lit a candle, because a candle is a quiet vow, not a performance, and watched the flame stand gold and certain against the dim. If someday you like lemon, I will learn to make it right. I will zest it by hand, so the whole house smells like brightness and summer.

And if someday you prefer chocolate, I will pretend it is not my favorite and let you take the bigger piece. That is what love really is. Not grand gestures, but a thousand quiet offerings.

The daily practice of giving, of choosing, of staying. Each small surrender is a rehearsal for the moment you might need me. And I am learning, slowly, that even the smallest act; a crooked cake, a flickering candle, can be its own kind of prayer.

✳ ⚬ ✳

Miles earned more, a little at a time. Enough to staple a paper schedule to the wall and call it a plan. Enough to pay a month ahead on the electric bill. Sufficient that the social worker he met twice no longer gave him a look as if he needed to apologize for existing. He kept receipts in an envelope he labeled "proof." It made no legal difference. Paper is not a cradle. But it changed something in him. The miles accumulated.

On a late spring afternoon, when the city finally remembered its blues, he saw her. The air smelled of sugar and grass, of the season trying to forgive itself for winter. The park was alive in that clumsy way only small-town fairs can be, with foldout tents in uneven rows, extension cords snaking through the trampled green, the hum of generators, and the hopeful laughter of children.

The band on the temporary stage was tuning their guitars, strings stretching into uncertain courage. He lifted tables, hammered stakes, coiled cables; simple work, honest work, the kind that left room for thought. Miles had learned, over the years, to live with his head down. Humility was not shame, he reminded himself, though the world often confused the two. He had grown used to seeing only what was in front of him. The next task, the next paycheck, the next reason to keep moving. That is why he did not notice her at first.

It came as sound before sight: a small, bell-clear laugh that reached him clean, unfiltered by the noise of the crowd. It was light itself finding a gap between leaves, something too pure to mistake for anything else. Miles' chest tightened. For a heartbeat, he stood still, hands resting on the edge of a wooden table, the air holding him like a question. It could be any child, he told himself. The park was full of faces painted like dinos and fairies, hands sticky with lemonade, shoes scuffed with joy.

It could be anyone. He forced himself back to work, untangling a cord, adjusting a pole, pretending the sound had not reached the deepest part of him. He told himself not to look. But love, even when buried, recognizes its own voice. The laugh came again; closer now, bubbling up like a song that refused to be forgotten. Against his will, he turned and glanced. And there she was.

Eleanor was there in a stroller beneath a tree, hands reaching for the sun-glitter in the leaves. Her hair had more brown in it than he remembered, though memory is a liar, and he had no right to rely on it. Eleanor's cheeks still had the fullness of the moon. There was a smudge at the corner of her mouth — frosting. She wore a yellow dress.

Miles wanted to believe that meant something, that somewhere the universe had agreed to soften the edges for this afternoon. Lydia's red appeared at his periphery, off to the side in a circle of women with sunglasses and the kind of laughter meant to be heard. He stepped behind a pillar of the bandstand and watched his daughter watch the world: fat bees visiting clover, a dog dragging a man who pretended not to be dragged, and a boy in a blue shirt that said TRY AGAIN.

Eleanor clapped for nothing and everything at once. He would remember this for twelve years. He did not approach. Courage is not a weapon you can aim at innocence without damage. He pressed his hand flat against the bandstand pillar and counted his breaths. He listened to the bass guitar tune itself into something like a heartbeat. He imagined walking out, kneeling beside her, and saying, "Hello there, I'm no one to you but I love you." Miles imagined Lydia's mouth as a blade, and the security guard's hand, and the policeman's pen, and the judge's frown sighing into its old shape.

He turned away, walked to the far side of the park, and moved a stack of chairs that did not need moving. He stayed until the shadows grew longer than his doubt. When he finally went home, he opened the shoe box and wrote until the light failed. He wrote what he had seen: the yellow dress, the frosting mouth, the bee, the boy's blue shirt with its stubborn instruction. Try again.

Summer laid a heat over the city that made even the bricks sweat. He learned the language of the oscillating fan, how to place it so the night could be held. He picked up extra shifts and saved for a lawyer who might someday teach him the shape of visitation. He learned to refuse certain kinds of tiredness. The grocery manager liked him.

"You're quiet," she said, which in retail meant you are
not making my days harder. She started giving him the
bakery's end-of-day bread. He took home loaves wrapped
in paper, touched by the dark in a way that made them taste
like a blessing. Miles learned to slice them thin, toast them
crisp, and eat them with tomatoes and salt when tomatoes
were cheap. He learned to enjoy what arrived.

In August, for the first time, he allowed himself to sit at
the kitchen table with a sheet of paper drawn. He had never
been a man for lines; his hands were better at lifting than
tracing, but he wanted to make her a book someday. A book
about a door that stayed open no matter how many winds
knocked at it. He made doors in pencil, doors with brass
knobs smudged by hands, doors whose light leaked from
underneath. He drew a set of stars in the corner of one page;
three points, then five, then the kind of star children draw,
with intersecting lines that look like guidance.

He felt foolish and free at once. He later took the
drawings to the pastor. "I think it might be a children's
book," he said, embarrassed by his own voice. The pastor
studied it as if it were holy writ. "It already is," you started
with the truth." He said. "What is the truth?" Miles asked.
"That a door can be a promise. We have that little fair in
October. You could set up a table. Sell your door drawings,
write people's names above them as blessings.
You're good with wood. Maybe make a few frames."
The pastor smiled. "I'm not..." He began to say. The pastor
said, "Good? Who asked you to be perfect? Be faithful."
He later started building frames out of pallet wood, even
though the smell of the wood sometimes called him back
to that courthouse bench, the varnish the same, the echo the
same. Miles sanded until splinters turned to silk.

He painted the edges blue and left the wood's face bare
and hand-lettered lines he had written at the kitchen table:

*A door does not love you less because it is closed. It is
a door either way. One day, when you turn the knob, it will
remember that it is also a way through.*

The October fair arrived with gold light poured from
a low sun, with burners warming cider that smelled like
apology and forgiveness. He sold three frames and gave
away two. An elderly man handed him a twenty and said,
"For the girl." Miles did not ask which girl; he must have
seen it in the way the letter-maker looked at doors. The bill
went into a jar labeled visitation. Nights thinned into early
winter. He volunteered at the food pantry to learn the names
of those who were good at surviving. He took a class on
tenants' rights at the community center and learned to speak
in sentences that were not excuses.

He learned to say, "I can do Tuesday morning," and
mean it. He learned to say, "No," when a friend with
familiar eyes offered him a bottle that would make the
hours disappear. On her second birthday, he did not bake
a cake. He took the bus to the planetarium on a free day
and sat under a dome painted with a universe too faithful
to be real. When the guide dimmed the lights and the stars
revealed themselves in their printed precision, he tilted
his head back, mouth slightly open, and thought of how,
somewhere, Eleanor might be looking up at the same sky,
learning how the constellations are made from lines we
agree to see.

Miles heard three names that stuck that day; Aquila, Lyra, Cygnus, and wrote them down for a bedtime story he kept rehearsing.

✶ ⚷ ✶

My little star,

When you were born, I did not know the names of the ones above us. I just knew they existed. Steady, unbothered, older than anything I could understand.

You came the same way they did, suddenly and without permission, burning your small light into my sky and rearranging everything I thought I knew about the dark.

Tonight, I learned one of their names: Aquila. The eagle. They say he carries lightning for the gods, which feels like a strange job for a creature that was meant to fly freely. But I suppose we all carry something for someone, don't we? Some of us carry letters. Some of us carry silence. Some of us carry guilt until it becomes a shape we can live beside.

If I ever bring you anything, I hope it is not thundering. God knows there has been enough noise in the space between us. I wish instead to bring you a calm room. One with a door that knows your hand, where you do not have to knock to be let in. I want to be in that room. I want you to know you can come to me, even if it takes years, even if you have forgotten the address.

But if I must bring lightning, let it be the kind that shows you where to land. The kind that splits the sky, not in anger, but in clarity, so that even in the storm, you will know which direction carries your name.

I saw an eagle tonight as I left the planetarium. Just a shadow against the streetlights, wings catching a current I could not see. It vanished into the dark as if swallowed by it, but I kept my eyes on the spot where it disappeared.

That is what loving you feels like sometimes: watching something beautiful vanish into the distance and still refusing to look away. I miss you in ways I do not know how to name.

That is why I am learning the stars, so I can borrow their language until I find my own.

Always,
Dad

✳ ⚷ ✳

Between the lines, he told the truth that he believed. That maybe he had not fought hard enough, had not been ready or had not been enough; not then, maybe not ever in the way a young father dreams he might be. Miles had imagined that love could outweigh circumstance, that a heart full of devotion could stand before a judge and make a case all on its own. But love, he learned, is not legal tender. It buys nothing in rooms where words like "custody" and "stability" replace mercy. Shame became his inheritance, the only thing he could claim without paperwork. It followed him into every job, every quiet night, every mirror he tried not to investigate.

At first, he carried it like a wound. Tender, visible, something that demanded tending. But years have a way of teaching you what will not heal. So, he began to carry it differently. Not to hide it, but to hold it. Like a stone in his pocket: small enough to live with, heavy enough to never forget. Sometimes he would reach for it without realizing. When standing in line at the grocery store or watching other fathers swing their children at the park, his fingers would close around it as though by reflex. That quiet pressure reminded him of everything he once failed to do, and everything he still hoped to make right.

It was his penance, yes, but also his compass: proof that he had not gone numb. On the worst nights, he would take the stone out, figuratively or otherwise, and set it on the table beside him. Miles studied it the way some men study scripture, turning it in the lamplight, tracing its edges until the shame softened into understanding. It was still there, but so was he. That counted for something. He promised the air, God, the ribbon, or the ghostly weight of her head that still lived in the crook of his arm, that he would never ask her to forgive him just to make his life easier.

He would never trade her pain for his peace. If forgiveness ever came, it had to be hers, uncoerced and unclaimed. His task was more straightforward, harder: to stay. To build something steady enough that, if Eleanor ever came looking, she would find not a man begging for absolution, but a man who had finally learned how to stand still and wait with the light on.

When the second winter's first rain came to Sierra Mesa, Arizona, Miles stood at the window and watched the city quietly turn silver. Rain was the truest kind of grace in Sierra Mesa; rare but never forgotten. It did not erase the noise or the struggle; it softened them, turned them human again. The gutters, choked so long with dust, found their voices. The red clay roofs darkened to wine.

The streets, usually brittle under the sun, exhaled the scent of petrichor. That sweet, living perfume of earth remembering water. Outside his window, the alley below transformed. The cat that had meowed for weeks fell silent, taking shelter somewhere unseen. The dented dumpsters, loud and ordinary, gleamed faintly as if someone had polished their edges. Rain streaked down the cracked brick walls, carrying the desert's tired dust into small rivers that curled along the curb.

It was a softer world for an hour; the kind that makes a man stop pretending he has grown used to loneliness. Miles pressed a palm to the cool glass, watching the beads of water race each other down the pane. Each droplet caught a fragment of light from the streetlamp and bent it into gold before slipping away. He thought of how life does that, too; holds brightness for a moment before it falls. Inside, the apartment smelled of wet air and old coffee.

The leaky corner of the ceiling ticked steadily into a bucket with a rhythm he had come to accept like the heartbeat of a house trying to keep him company. The sound was oddly comforting. It was proof that the world was still moving, that even in its smallest ways, it was still alive. The rain softened everything it touched: the nail head blushing through his warped floorboard, the cracks in the windowsill where wind used to whistle through and steal his sleep. It even softened him, the edges of his exhaustion, the sharpness of old disappointments.

He stood there for a long time, breathing in the smell of wet earth and asphalt and faint, dying smoke from the diner's sign across the street. In Sierra Mesa, the rain never lasted long; the sky was stingy that way. But while it fell, it made everything glisten. Even the broken things. Especially the broken stuff. He closed his eyes and let the sound of it fill him until the noise inside quieted, too. For the first time in a long time, he did not feel forgotten.

He had twenty-six dollars in the Visitation jar, a few crumpled bills, and a handful of coins that clinked like fragile hope whenever he counted them. Beside it sat the shoe box with thirty-two letters folded inside, each one a timestamp of faith. They were uneven, some pages stained with coffee, some spotted by tears, but all of them written with the same steady devotion.

He sometimes wondered if the letters were more prayer than ink. He filled the kettle with tap water, its slow groan echoing through the small apartment. The stove clicked three times before the flame caught, blue and sure. When the water began to hiss, he leaned against the counter and watched the steam rise, curling upward until it slivered the air. In that soft light, the room almost looked holy. Miles thought about how faith works.

How sometimes it is not belief in miracles or prayers, it is just the act of staying. Of making tea. Of lighting the same candle every night, even when no one is there to see it. Outside, a child's laughter carried through the bright rain, skipping sound between the soft percussion of drops. He smiled faintly, though his eyes stung. He imagined her out there somewhere, splashing barefoot through puddles, watching the streetlights shimmer in the wet pavement while wearing a yellow raincoat instead of the red that haunted his memories.

The whistle of the kettle pulled him back. He poured the water over a tired tea bag and watched the color bloom, slow and amber, like warmth remembering its way back into the world. The steam rose in gentle spirals, brushing his face, dampening the edges of thought. He sat by the window and held the mug between his palms, the heat grounding him.

The rain kept falling, steady now, painting the alley into something kind. The streetlight outside rippled in the puddles like a small sun learning to breathe again. Miles thought of the letters waiting in their box, the ones that began with *My little star* and never stopped reaching. He thought of all the words he had not yet written, all the ones that kept him tethered to the idea of her.

He did not know when he would see her. He did not know if he ever would. But as the night deepened and the city quieted beneath its curtain of rain, he felt something small and specific settle in his chest, something like peace. Not the peace of an answer or peace of arrival. The peace that comes from choosing to stay anyway. *"Hold fast,"* he said to no one. *"Try again."* Miles stopped keeping count of small humiliations.

There were too many, and they had started to repeat themselves anyway; the landlord's pause before accepting rent in crumpled bills, the sideways glance of a clerk when he handed over a food voucher, the way people's eyes slid past him when they didn't want to imagine how thin their own safety nets might be. He learned to let them pass. To treat them like weather. Instead, he started keeping track of small mercies.

The bus driver waited for an extra half-block while he sprinted through the cold in boots that had long forgotten waterproofing. The woman at the laundromat showed him how to untangle a twisted sheet without losing patience. The grocery manager pointed to the small envelope on payday and said, *"You're getting there,"* as if there were a real place, not heaven, not success, just a room with curtains you could choose yourself.

Miles noticed how mercy worked in disguise: a stranger's nod, a warm hand steadying the door, the last piece of bread at the church pantry left untouched as if meant for him. They were not miracles, not in the biblical sense, but they were proof that goodness still passed quietly from hand to hand, surviving the noise.

★ ✪ ★

In spring, he took a day off. He had not meant to; it just happened. He woke to light pouring through the thin curtain, and for once, he did not rush to chase the day. Miles packed a peanut butter and banana sandwich, drizzled with honey, the way his dad enjoyed it, and wrapped it in foil. He then walked to the river, the place where the city pretended to be a small town, where concrete gave way to grass. The bridge narrowed into the sky's blue reflection. The geese were there, rude and magnificent, claiming the bank with bad manners and perfect feathers.

Their noise filled the air with a strange kind of confidence. He sat with his back against a slick-barked tree, the roots pressing into his spine like a reminder that even stillness can have structure. From his coat pocket, he pulled out a secondhand copy of *Mrs. Dalloway* he had found at a thrift store. The pages smelled faintly of dust and rain. He stumbled through the sentences, the way they rippled and curved like water, saying more in their rhythm than in their meaning.

He had learned something there he could not have named aloud: that a person could inhabit a single moment so completely it expanded, making space for every other. That living did not always mean chasing, fixing, or explaining. Sometimes it meant sitting under a tree, watching the river carry everything you have lost downstream, and letting it.

Miles learned that grief and joy were not enemies but companions, like two hands carrying the same fragile cup. That love could live in both. That one could make the other bearable. And as the day stretched long, the sky slow and generous, he felt something he had not done in years. Not happiness. Not yet. But presence.

The ability to sit inside the ache and still see beauty threading through it. A soft wind came off the water, smelling faintly of rain and earth. He tilted his head back and closed his eyes, feeling the sunlight through his eyelids, the way it painted the world red and gold from behind. For a moment, he let himself believe that the world could be kind. That Eleanor was out there somewhere, laughing, whole. That he had not missed everything after all.

Distant cousins who stood together at the edge of every ordinary day; grief and joy, inseparable, sharing a language he was only just beginning to understand. Miles closed the book and sat there for a long time, the river moving slowly beside him, the sound of water brushing stones like breath. The sunlight had thinned to amber, and the air carried that fragile promise spring makes to remember how to break it.

Somewhere behind him, a child laughed, and he almost turned to look before he stopped himself. He knew better than chasing memories. From the inside pocket of his coat, he pulled a sheet of paper, creased, soft, already half-lived in and smoothed it against his knee.

The wind kept tugging at the edges, but he pressed it flat with the heel of his hand and began to write. It was not a letter, not really. It was more like a confession or a prayer that had disguised itself as a paragraph. His handwriting faltered once, then steadied.

✳ ⊶ ✳

My little star,

One day, you will ask me why I did not knock on every door in the city until you opened.

One day, you will ask why I did not shout loud enough for the entire world to hear your name. One day, you will ask why I did not fight the judge with more than words and empty pockets.

And I will not hide behind metaphors or miracles. I will not make your mother into a villain just to make myself a hero.

I will tell you the truth. I was poor. I was scared. I was too young to know that fear and love can live in the same body and still not cancel each other out. I thought strength meant waiting until I was enough. Until I could bring you into a life that did not leak at the corners, that did not shake in the wind. But I mistook waiting for patience, and patience for love. The world told me about the safest place for you.

For them, it was not with me. And I believed it. Because when you love someone that fiercely, you learn to call surrender a kind of protection. If I was wrong, and God, I was, I will carry that wrong the way a person holds their own name. It's carved into me. It is mine.

But I never put you down. Not once.

Even when my hands were empty, they remembered the weight of you. Even when the years stretched too wide, I walked through them as if carrying something invisible but real, a small heartbeat in my palm.

✳ ⚍ ✳

Miles paused, the pen hovering above the page, its tip trembling just enough to betray him. The sky had turned the color of bruised peaches, the light folding in on itself the way it does before night admits defeat. A few stars had already begun their small rebellions against the fading blue; fragile, trembling, brave.

He stared at the half-written words and felt the ache rise like a tide in his throat. It was not just sadness; sadness was clean, temporary. This was heavier. This was the kind of ache that settles into your bones until you forget what they weighed before.

He thought of how some truths can only be looked at in pieces, because taken whole, they could burn you blind. Like sunlight fractured across water, too bright to bear, too honest to deny. The river had caught the dying sun and thrown it back in a thousand small shivers. Each reflection broke before it reached him. Each one was a truth he could touch but never hold. He watched it for a long time, the light, the motion, the beautiful futility of it all.

It reminded him of a memory, how it promises to take you home, only to leave you standing on the shore, holding a version of the past that never learned how to come back. Miles thought of her; the curve of her small head, the weight of her heartbeat against his chest once, the life that had gone on without him. The distance between them was not measured in miles anymore but in moments he had not been allowed to live. He could almost hear her laughing in the water's rush.

And for a terrible second, he nearly turned, as if Eleanor might be there. But the wind moved through him, empty and cold, and he remembered himself. In his mind, he saw the door again, the one he had always imagined between them. It stood the same as ever, solid and merciless, but the light had changed. Along the edges, he saw gold; thin, trembling, alive. Someone inside had lit a candle and forgotten to blow it out.

The thought nearly undid him. He folded the page with care, the paper softening under the heat of his hands. Miles slipped it into his jacket pocket, close to his heart, because where else could he keep what he could not say aloud? The river murmured on, unconcerned, carrying the day away piece by piece. The world, as always, refused to stop for heartbreak. It had no reason to.

He stood there anyway, rooted, exhausted, unwilling to look away from the living proof that things could move and still be broken. When he finally spoke, his voice was more breath than sound. *"Not yet open,"* he whispered, *"but not locked."* The words hung in the air, thin as thread, but strong enough to hold him upright. For the first time in an exceedingly long while, it did not feel like surrender. It felt like faith. And for him, that was enough.

He went home, worked another shift, slept, woke, wrote, built, saved, and learned to be the kind of man he had promised the air he would become. He did not know when the door would open. He only knew his part: to wait by it without bitterness, to keep his hand warm for the knob. On the night that would become a story, a summer evening still far from the day Eleanor would be old enough to choose, he took the shoe box down and counted the letters. Sixty-eight. Enough to tell him the habit had outgrown its beginning.

He laid them on the table like place settings for a meal that had not yet been made and set the ribbon on top, pale yellow against the sifted brown of envelopes rubbed smooth by years. Miles turned on the lamp. The room breathed its small gold. When he closed his eyes, he saw her in a yellow dress smudged with frosting, laughing at leaves. He heard an old bass guitar tuning itself into readiness and smelled bread that had traveled the day to arrive in his hands, still tasting of generosity.

He felt again how the city could surprise a person with kindness. He placed a blank page in front of him and wrote a title before the salutation, though he had never done so before. *The Letter He Never Sent.* He crossed out *Never* and wrote *Not Yet.* He smiled at the correction and wrote the date in the corner then began. *My little star,* he wrote and then paused.

He felt the moment rise around him, light as steam from
a kettle, the kind that disappears before you can decide
whether to warm your hands or let it go. Ordinary as the
cracked vinyl of a bus seat, where strangers breathe the
same tired air and nobody says a word. And yet enormous,
and vast as a sky dome at the planetarium when the room
goes black, and the ceiling opens into forever. The hush
of that memory came back to him; a whole crowd falling
silent, the guide's voice dissolving into dark, and the slow
blooming of stars above, pinpricks first, then constellations,
then galaxies.

He remembered how the audience always gasped when
they realized how small they were. He felt that same
smallness now, standing at the edge of the river, caught
between the noise of the city behind him and the endless
quiet ahead. His life, with all its jagged edges and small
humiliations, had led to this still point where grief and
wonder shared the same breath. He was nobody remarkable.
Just a man with calloused hands and a pocket full of folded
paper, but in that moment, under the bruised sky, he felt tied
to everything.

The air shimmered, faintly alive. The sound of the water,
the distant hum of traffic, even the faint ache in his knee,
seemed to speak in one voice: *You are still here.*

Miles let that realization settle, fragile as steam, fleeting
as starlight, and whispered to himself, *"Keep still. Let your
eyes adjust."*

Miles began again.

✴ ๏ ✴

My little star,
*You are still far from reading this. I thought I understood
what impossible meant by now, but today it showed me
another version.*

*Not the kind of impossible I have learned to live with;
poverty like a long hallway, a judge like a door that does
not swing, but the other kind.*

*The kind where dawn finds a way through a city that was
forgotten, where a girl in a yellow dress laughs at leaves
because the world is teaching her joy, and Eleanor is letting
herself learn.*

*The kind where a father waits by a door for so long that
the waiting becomes a part of his body, and then one day he
hears the knob turn.*

✳  ✳

Miles stopped, put his pen down, and leaned back,
listening. Outside, someone called a name from a
window, and laughter fell like cut paper through the light.
Somewhere, a radio station found a love song and kept it.
Somewhere, a girl newly into her second year slept in a
room painted a color he could not guess, her breath steady
as a metronome, her mind untangling only the smallest
beginnings of a life Eleanor was still far from choosing. He
touched the ribbon and felt the page.

He touched the door frame on his way to bed, palm flat,
like a man who blesses thresholds. *"Happy birthday,"* he
whispered to the future, still years away, and already here.
"Happy birthday, my little star." Miles slept, and the dark,
no longer an enemy, gathered itself around him like a coat
someone had left on the back of his chair in case the night
turned cold.

38

Letters in Boxes

The years passed not as seasons, but as pages slipped into a box. Every letter began the same: *My little star.* Some were no more than a paragraph, written at the end of a long shift when his hands smelled of grease or bleach. Others filled page after page, words tumbling over each other like floodwaters breaking through. Miles wrote of nothing. Bread rising too fast in the oven, the neighbor's cat that had adopted his windowsill, the way frost clung to the inside of the glass until the sun pried it loose, and yet in the nothing was everything.

Because each word said, *I am still here. I have not forgotten you.* The shoe boxes grew heavier. First one, then two, then three, stacked like bricks against a wall he refused to believe was permanent. The cardboard softened over time, its corners blunted by years of being opened, overseen, and closed. Dust gathered in the seams like the world's quiet attempt to forget him, but he would not let it. He labeled each one carefully, in small, uneven letters: *Year 3. Year 4. Year 5.*

It was less for organization than for prayer; a way to mark the passage of love in a world that measured worth by pay stubs and signatures. He imagined them someday in her arms, not as proof of his goodness but as evidence of his staying. *"Here,"* he would say without words. *"Here is the time I spent loving you when I was not allowed to say your name aloud."*

He wondered sometimes what Eleanor would think when she opened them. *Would she recognize the handwriting, the places where tears had puckered the paper? Would she understand that absence had not been neglect but a kind of faith that was clumsy, constant, imperfect?*

He stacked the boxes against the wall beside his bed, their weight leaning toward him at night like a promise. Work never ceased. It could not. The world did not stop to let a man grieve himself back to wholeness. He carried crates in warehouses that smelled of oil and rain and swept aisles under flickering lights, pushing the broom like a slow metronome through silence. He hauled lumber until his shoulders learned to accept the sting, until the weight felt more familiar than rest.

At night, he washed dishes in the echoing dark of a diner long after the last customer had gone. The plates clinked like tired ghosts, and the smell of soap and burnt coffee settled into his skin. Steam curled around his face until it felt like he was dissolving into it. Jobs came and went like tides. Some kind, some cruel, but his body learned how to bend without breaking. He stopped asking for meaning in every task. The meaning was in the doing.

The ache in his back, the bruises across his palms, the calluses that split and healed again; each one was proof of endurance, and endurance was proof of love. He began to measure time not in months or paychecks, but in letters written, in candles burned down to nubs, in mornings where he woke and told himself, *Still here. Still trying.*

And when the work became too much, when exhaustion pressed its weight against his ribs and whispered that Eleanor would never know, he would open one of the shoe boxes, run his hand over the top letter, and feel the world steady. Each folded page was a heartbeat, stored and waiting. Each one said what the courts had not let him say: *I did not stop. I am still yours.*

On his daughter's sixth birthday, he bought a balloon from a street vendor.

A single red one, cheap and bright as a wound. The vendor asked if he wanted it tied to his wrist, but he shook his head. He tried to feel it in his hand, wanting the ribbon to leave its mark. He carried it through the city, weaving between strangers and storefronts, the wind tugging at it like a restless child. The ribbon burned against his palm, a thin white line of proof that he was still capable of holding something that wanted to rise.

Miles did not have a cake, or candles, or anyone to sing with, but the balloon was enough; a simple declaration that somewhere, love still existed. When he reached the bridge, the sun was already softening into evening, the sky lavender at the edges, the river below rippling with stolen light. He stood there for a long time, watching the water move, the balloon swaying gently at his side like a heart undecided.

He whispered, *"Happy birthday my little star,"* and let it go. It rose, quick and sure, slipping from his hand with a sound too small to name. It climbed into the sky until it became a scarlet star, a single pulse of color against the cooling blue. He watched until it disappeared, refusing to blink, afraid that if he looked away too soon, Eleanor might not see it.

He imagined her somewhere standing in a yard, or by a window, tilting her head at that sudden red glimmer, not knowing it was meant for her. She would smile without understanding why. She would not notice at all. But still, he hoped.

Because hope, he had learned, was just love that refused to go quiet.

★ ✪ ★

Loneliness was a steady companion. It waited for him at
the end of each workday, unhurried and patient, sitting in
the single chair pulled up to a table meant for two. It did not
mock or scold. It simply existed, taking its place beside him
like an old friend who had stopped needing conversation.
He tried not to name it. Naming made things real, and real
things could break you. So instead, he named the colors
in the room; the brown of the table, the gray of the light,
the blue that gathered in corners where the sun never quite
reached.

He turned those colors into metaphors, into something
gentler than truth. In his letters, he made the brown into
warmth, the gray into patience, the blue into faith. He told
her stories about skies and rivers and the color of love when
it is waiting. Sometimes he thought that was all writing
was: turning what you cannot survive into something you
can hold.

He wrote her a sentence the year prior that stuck with
him.

★ ⚬ ★

Today, the gray walls reminded me of clouds.
Clouds change. They never stay. Neither will this
distance.

★ ⚬ ★

It was the kind of sentence that felt too small for what it
carried. He wrote it anyway. Words did not always have to
hold the whole truth. Sometimes they only had to keep you
from drowning.

The church became his refuge, not because of faith at
first, but because it was warm and no one asked too many
questions.

He swept floors and stacked cans in the food pantry, folding donated clothes until his hands smelled faintly of starch and dust. The building always seemed to hum softly with pipes groaning, footsteps echoing from somewhere unseen, the air alive with the faint vibration of hymns that lingered long after services ended. He learned he found comfort in that hum, in the idea that some things keep singing even when no one is listening.

Soon, people began to know him not as the man who lost, but as the man who stayed. A quiet fixture. A reliable hand. They left him small offerings of trust: keys to lock up at night, a thermos of coffee, the unspoken grace of belonging without explanation. The pastor often nodded toward him and said, "Steadfast," as if that word were enough to build a life around. Miles did not argue. It was better than being alone. But steadfastness did not erase the longing. It only gave it structure.

At night, when the city hushed, he would sit on the edge of his bed and hold the baby ribbon between his fingers until the threads frayed thinner. He had worn it smoothly with touch, the same way prayer beads lose their sharpness from years of need. He never prayed the exact words twice, but his hands always moved the same; slowly, circular, desperate. Sometimes he dreamed of her.

Not as Eleanor was, because he had only fragments, but the weight of her, the sound she made before she learned words, but as he imagined she might be. In the dreams, she was always running. Through fields, through fog, through sunlight that made her hair fire. He would call to her, and she would laugh; that bell-clear sound that had haunted him since the fair. His legs would move, but never fast enough.

The air would thicken, his chest would tighten, and she would fade into brightness before he reached her. He would wake with his hands clenched, his chest aching, whispering apologies into the dark. Sometimes, he was not sure who he was apologizing to anymore. God, her, or the man he might have been if the world had given him more time.

The letters grew wiser as the years pulled him forward.

In the beginning, they were filled with promises, frantic and bright:

✳ ⊶ ✳

I will see you soon. I will find a way.

✳ ⊶ ✳

Later, the words softened, stripped down to truth and endurance.

✳ ⊶ ✳

I do not know when this will change, but I believe it will. I will be waiting. You will never open the door and find me gone.

✳ ⊶ ✳

Miles learned that hope did not always roar. Sometimes it whispered. Sometimes it took the shape of a folded letter, a half-empty jar labeled *Visitation,* or a man sweeping a church floor long after the candles had gone out. And somewhere in those quiet rituals, he began to understand that faith is not a thing you hold in, it is what keeps you when you have let go of everything else.

On her seventh birthday, he added something new. Until then, the letters had been his own voice; clumsy, honest, threaded with hope. But that year, he began copying poems onto the backs of the pages, as if love needed a chorus. Yeats, Dickinson, Neruda. Voices that had outlived their bodies.

He wanted her to inherit not only his words, but the
words of those who had carried love through centuries of
light and loss. He wrote slowly, in careful script, so Eleanor
could read them when she was older, when her heart was
ready to recognize its own shape in someone else's.

He thought that she would find them one day and realize
that love, even when separated by years, could still be
fluent. One night, after finishing *To the Lighthouse,* he sat
with his candle flickering low and wrote in the margin of a
page meant for her.

* ⚬ *

*Life is made of lighthouses, moments of sudden
brightness against long seas of darkness. You are my
lighthouse, though you do not know it yet. You have kept me
from drowning more times than you will ever imagine.*

* ⚬ *

Miles paused before folding the letter, his pen still warm
in his hand. He then realized he was no longer writing
to convince her to know him, but to remind himself that
Eleanor existed. That she was somewhere, living, growing,
laughing beyond his reach. The world changed around him.
Neighbors moved out and did not come back. Buildings he
had known since his twenties came down one by one, their
absences filling the skyline like pulled teeth.

The city built new trains that roared through the night,
shaking his windowpanes and rearranging his dreams. But
his ritual never faltered. Candles almost every birthday.
Write a letter each week. Work each day. Hope each night.
He lived by those four commandments as though they were
sacred. On the worst nights, when his pay ran short and his
bones ached from hours of lifting and washing and bending,
he would strike a match and light the candle anyway.

It was never about the light. It was about the act; the quiet defiance of a man who refused to let love die in the dark.

★ ✪ ★

By the time Eleanor was nine, he had saved enough to hire a lawyer. The appointment was circled in red ink on his calendar for weeks, a minor miracle of courage. He ironed his shirt the night before, scrubbed his hands clean, and told himself he looked like a man who might be believed. The office smelled of leather and lemon polish; the kind of clean that felt expensive. The lawyer was young, his suit too fine for someone who could not yet hide his boredom. He listened as the father explained his case: the years, the letters, the lost birthdays. Miles tried to keep his voice even, but it wavered when he said her name. The lawyer tapped a pen against the desk and asked questions in a flat tone, as if filling out a form.

"Visitation, might be possible. But the mother, she will fight it." He said at last. *"She's always fought it,"* the father whispered. The lawyer sighed, looking at the papers spread between them. "Then you need more than love. You need proof of stability. A home. Consistent income. Insurance. Can you provide that?" He did not answer right away. He thought of his shoe boxes, many stacked high, years of devotion pressed into them like blueprints for a house he had never been able to build. He wanted to tell the man that he did have proof, that love was the most stable thing he had ever known, that his letters were the beams and boards of something strong enough to last a lifetime.

But paper hearts were not legal documents, and love did not count as collateral. He left the office with his jaw tight, his throat raw, and his hands buried deep in his pockets. The door clicked softly behind him, the kind of sound that pretends it is not a goodbye. Outside, the city was all noise and motion, but he moved through it slowly, carrying his silence like a fragile thing. The streets smelled of rain and diesel. The courthouse clock chimed the hour, impersonal and exact. Miles thought about what the lawyer had said, "proof of stability," and almost laughed.

Stability was a myth invented by people who had never had to lose everything just to keep one promise alive. He walked until his legs ached, until his anger dulled into something quieter, something that almost resembled peace. When he reached the bridge, he stopped and whispered, *"Still holding on,"* as if saying it aloud could make time listen. Then he went home, lit his candle, and followed the habit. That night, he almost did not write a letter. He sat at the table with a blank page in front of him and stared at it until the lamp's light swam into a blur.

The silence pressed hard that night, but eventually he found his way. Slowly, deliberately, he wrote:

✳ ☞ ✳

My little star,
Today I almost gave up.
The world felt too heavy, and the hours asked for more than I had to give. But then I remembered the sound of your laugh under the tree that day in the park.
How it rose, light and certain, as if joy itself had borrowed your voice. I remembered how yellow looked on you, how it made the whole sky seem kinder. And I knew I could not stop. Not today. Not ever.

✳ ☞ ✳

Miles folded the page, slid it into the box, and lit another candle. The flame flickered once, then steadied. Outside, winter brushed the city white again. He thought of doors. Always doors. Some are still locked; some are just waiting for the right hand.

And he whispered to the quiet: *"Try again. Always, try again."*

A Father's Devotion

By sheer luck and patient research, Miles learned the hours when the school opened itself to the town, the choir concerts with programs printed in inky purple, the art shows where canvases leaned like shy children against folding easels, the spring fair when the gym smelled of popcorn and scuffed varnish. Those were the nights he allowed himself to exist in her world. Public meant safe. Public meant no one could accuse him of trespassing for loving his own child. Public meant he could stand at the back, become another shadow in a room full of them, and ask for nothing of the universe but a glimpse.

He told himself it was enough. It had to be. On a November night when the air thinned to glass, he took a seat in the last row of the auditorium The curtain was red, the same red he had trained himself not to hate. Red like courtrooms. Red like goodbye. Still, under the stage lights, it glowed softer, almost edible, as if memory had finally sweetened what it once burned. Along the proscenium, someone had draped garland that sagged in the middle, heavy with paper snowflakes and silver tinsel.

A string of lights blinked in a stubborn pattern, one bulb dead, another too bright, like a town insisting on cheer with whatever it had left. A plastic wreath hung crooked near the side curtain, and the smell of pine cleaner clung to the aisle like someone had tried to scrub the year down to something new.

Miles kept his eyes on the stage anyway. Holiday decorations always felt like a public promise. Warmth on display. A reminder that most people had somewhere to go after the applause.

The seats filled slowly with parents brushing hair from their children's foreheads, hands smoothing ribbons, murmurs thick with pride. He kept his head low, the program open on his lap but unread. His hands had learned a way of stillness that could pass for calm, though inside him, something small and wild paced in circles. The band began to tune. The lights dimmed. He felt the shift in the air, that hush before something holy begins.

Then Eleanor walked out. Miles did not need the program to find her. He would have known her anywhere, with the way she moved, half-serious, half-wonder. The way her hair caught the light and refused to let it go. She took her place among the others, but his heart did not know *among*. It only knew *there*. Eleanor lifted her chin, ready to sing, and in that single movement, he felt every year between them collapse. He did not clap. He did not cry. He just sat there, still as prayer, whispering to no one: *"There you are."*

When the lights dimmed, the chatter fell into a single breath shared by a hundred throats. The air changed with the kind of change you can feel more than see, like a heartbeat before a confession. The choir filled out in black: shirts starched, skirts swinging in careful arcs, each child a slight silhouette of someone's hope. The stage lights painted their faces in soft amber, halos for the ordinary. He scanned the line, eyes restless, searching.

He looked for her in a sea of sameness; faces washed in the same shine of youth and nerves, but he found her by her hands. He had always imagined that it is how he would recognize her, not by her face but by some smaller human gesture that the world did not teach her to hide. Eleanor worried the hem of her cuff the way a child might twist a secret between their fingers, shaping an invisible thread.

When she smiled, it was shy and brief, as if happiness
had to ask for permission. She pressed her knuckle to her
lip before letting it go, and there was the same minor quirk
he had once seen in a face no bigger than his forearm. She
is taller now. Older. Her hair, pinned half-back, was the
color of brown sugar left too long in a jar on a windowsill,
catching the light in slow, golden flecks. He tried to imagine
what her voice would sound like now, deeper perhaps,
shaped by all the years he had missed.

Then the first notes rose, thin as a new moon, and the
room shifted. Her mouth opened, and music filled the air.
He did not hear the words; they dissolved before they
reached him. He did not need them. The sound of her was
its own language, geography he had been tracing blindly
since the beginning. Every note mapped a place he had once
dreamed of reaching. Every breath reminded him how far
he still was. Something in him broke and mended at once.

He wanted to close his eyes, but he could not. He wanted
to look forever. And so, he sat there, perfectly still, with
tears threatening but unspent, feeling the miracle and the
punishment of being near her but not known. He sat for
three songs, then four. He folded the program along its
spine, then unfolded it, then folded it again to keep his
hands busy.

He thought of the shoe boxes at home stacked neatly
against the wall, each one heavy with folded paper and
years. The numbers had stopped mattering. The weight had
not, with each letter a small brick laid against the cold. If
you believed hard enough, you could build shelter out of
anything: cardboard, candlelight, words. He had built his
whole house out of her name. He had promised himself
rules.

They were simple, merciless things: Never closer than
a room's length. Never, ever, a word. Leave before the last
applause. The heart, he had learned, can be trained into
obedience that looks so much like love it fools even the one
carrying it. He stayed seated as people around him began
to stir. Programs rustled. Someone behind him whispered
about missed notes and proud grandparents. A father two
rows ahead leaned close to his daughter and adjusted the
bow at her collar, his hands careful, reverent, as if touching
something breakable.

The gym carried the layered scent of sugar and wet
wool, cocoa cooling in paper cups, the faint metallic tang
of folding chairs. Laughter rose and fell in uneven bursts.
Small rituals unfolded in the aisles: mittens tugged off
with teeth, scarves shaken loose, cheeks kissed without
ceremony. Miles watched it all from his seat, half-shadow,
half-man. He folded the program again until it was a small,
perfect square in his hand. The lights brightened, and the
crowd stretched like something waking up. Applause rose
in a sudden swell, then softened into movement as people
shifted in their seats.

Miles stood then, not trusting himself to stay. He slipped
through the side door before the second half could begin.
Outside, the night breathed rain. Not a storm. Just the
steady kind, falling in fine silver threads that found every
surface and made it shimmer.

The air was cool and clean, scented faintly of wet earth
and distant creosote, the smell of Arizona remembering
it could still be green. The streetlights hummed, halos
bending through the drizzle. Puddles formed at the base of
the curb, catching fragments of light and breaking them into
trembling gold. The trees along the sidewalk glistened, their
bare limbs jeweled with droplets.

He looked back once. The door was still open, the glow
of the gym spilling out onto the wet pavement. Through it,
he could hear the muffled rise of chatter and music, laughter
folded into the hum of the world continuing without him.
He stood in the rain long enough for it to soak through his
shoulders, long enough for it to cool the ache that lived just
behind his ribs.

Then he turned away, the sound of applause beginning
to swell inside. He left before it could reach him, because
leaving while the door was still open hurt less than waiting
for it to close.

Miles went home, lit his candle, and wrote.

✻ ☛ ✻

My little star,

Tonight, I heard you sing.

*Forgive me. I was at the back, far, as I should be. The
light reached you, not me, and that felt right.*

*I did not clap for you, though my hands ached to. I did
not want to steal a single echo meant for you. I did not want
to make a wish that was not mine to make.*

*But I saw you. I saw the way your hands move before
your mouth does, how they speak their own small language,
nervous, tender, full of music before a sound is made. They
are my hands, I think.*

*Or I learned mine from you. Sometimes gestures are the
only inheritance that never asks for permission.*

*Your voice carried across the room like light underwater,
bent, distant, but still reaching. You sang the way I once
dreamed of living: honest, unafraid, unaware of who might
be listening.*

*And when I heard you breathe between verses, I realized
something I had not understood in eleven years: that
language can be both a place and a bridge. You stood on
both tonight.*

53

You built something I could finally cross, if only for a moment. I walked away at the break. Not because I wanted to, but because I needed to. I want the first time you see me to be your choice, not an accident, not a shadow that happens to be mine.

I want to stand before you only when your heart says yes. If you ever wonder whether someone in the back row loved you, someone who did not clap, who left early, who kept his eyes down but his soul wide open. The answer is yes. Always yes. You were magnificent.

Always,

Dad

✳ ⚷ ✳

The page trembled a little under his pen, but not from cold. It was the tremor of a man trying to hold still while his heart remembered how to move. The ink caught the light, wet and uncertain, before settling into the paper like something accepting its fate. When he finished, he sat for a long time, staring at the last line as though it might open into something larger: some answer, some release. It did not. It was just a line on paper. But it was his line, and that was enough. Miles folded the letter carefully, as one might manage a fragile photograph, and slipped it into the envelope marked *Year 11*.

The box was complete now. He wondered what weight love had when measured in paper and ink. It could be the same weight as silence. That could be why both could feel unbearable. He turned off the lamp. The click sounded final, but not cruel. The room fell into darkness, and he sat there, letting his eyes learn the shape of things again: the faint outline of the chair, the window, the narrow bed. The slow emergence of the familiar. It reminded him of the planetarium.

The way the lights dimmed, and the guide always said, "Give it time, your eyes will find the stars." So, he waited. Edges first, then corners, then the quiet middle where everything ordinary lived. The room became itself again, piece by piece. And in that slow returning of shape, he felt something loose like grief exhaling. He thought of her voice again, soft, and clear, and let it linger once more before the dark carried it away.

Then he whispered into the quiet, *"Goodnight, my little star,"* and waited for the silence to answer.

Eleanor sang that night because the music teacher, a woman who wore her silver hair like a crown and her bracelets like bells, had told the choir to sing through their bones. *"Not from the throat, not from the chest; through the bones,"* she whispered to herself, tapping her wrist against her heart so the bracelet chimed like tiny applause. "Let the sound live where your soul lives," she told them. "If it only passes through your mouth, it will forget where it came from. But if it travels through your bones, it will remember you."

The children had giggled at first, exchanging glances that seemed to signal she was strange but kind, the way children always do with adults who dare to speak like poets. But when the first note rose, something changed. The air itself seemed to pause, listening. From the back of the room, he watched his daughter tilt her head just slightly, as if evaluating the idea. Then Eleanor sang. And when she did, it was not from her throat at all. It was deeper, older, as though something inside her had been waiting for permission.

The sound filled the small auditorium, warm and sure, and for a moment, the stage lights softened around her. He thought about what it sounded like to sing through your bones. How maybe that is all life ever was: carrying the song of those who came before you, vibrating with every story you did not get to tell. He wondered if she knew that in that instant, she was singing for the part of him that had no voice, and the part of her that did not yet know why the music felt so familiar.

It was the first time she could remember she had felt something inside her answer her aloud, even if she could not hear it. "Not just throat," the teacher had said in rehearsal, tapping her own sternum with one ringed finger. "Not just mouth. Bones. Let the song sit where grief sits. Let joy vibrate your ribs. Otherwise, it's just notes. We are not making notes. We're making memories."

She held the memory of words the way some people held the backs of chairs. She did not know why that was. Only that sound seemed to steady her more than anything else. At home, language felt like glass held up to the light, only to be smeared. Her mother could be sugar, yes, when neighbors watched, but sugar that cut the tongue. And *Father* was a word she had learned to search with her teeth as if it might have a crack.

On stage, under the warm lights, she could open her mouth and give the room something that was not an argument. She liked that. She liked the breath before sound, the slight hush where every person in the audience was an unstruck match. At intermission, Eleanor stepped into the lobby and found the noise too bright. The air buzzed with relief and sugar, with people talking too loudly simply because they could.

The tables were crowded with paper cups and half-eaten cookies, with hands gesturing and laughter overlapping. Everywhere she looked, there was movement. Mothers refastening coats, fathers clapping shoulders, students flushed with the afterglow of being seen. She stood for a moment, feeling the room's pulse and not knowing how to match it. The noise pressed against her skin, warm but weighty, a tide of small happinesses that did not seem to include her. The cocoa smelled too sweet. The steam curled into her face like breath she had not asked for.

She found herself wishing for a bit of space, a quiet little corner to collect herself, but quiet was rare in rooms made of pride. Her friend Leah appeared beside her, smiling with the easy confidence of someone who belonged wherever Eleanor stood. She squeezed her arm twice, quick, as if to lend her borrowed steadiness, a silent *"you were terrific, you are okay, stay here with me."*

She nodded and smiled back, but her eyes drifted past the tables, toward the double doors that led outside. Beyond them, through the glass, she could see the rain-slick streetlights burning softly against the night. The blacktop shone like a mirror, the puddles trembling each time a drop fell. For reasons she could not name, she wanted to step into it. Not to run, not to hide; just to breathe air that had not already been shaped by other people's stories.

Leah tugged her sleeve, asking if she wanted more cocoa. She shook her head. Her voice came out small, steady, and practiced. "I'm good." But the truth was, she was not sure what "good" meant. Her gaze found the doors again. Through the rippling reflection of the glass, she thought, just for a breath, that she saw someone there. A shape, still and waiting. A coat darkened by rain.

A presence that felt like memory wearing a new face. And then it was gone. She blinked, and the world rushed back to noise, the chatter of parents, the laughter of students, the scrape of chairs against the varnished floor. Only the rain stayed soft against the windows, steady and sure, as if it knew something she did not yet have words for. "You were beautiful," Leah said. She rolled her eyes, but softly. "We were in tune," she said. "That's all." Her mother appeared with a poinsettia, red. Of course, red.

The kind of red that announced itself, that never had to ask permission to be seen. Its leaves were edged in gold foil, its bow too large, too certain. "Smile," she said, without looking at her. It was not a request, just a reflex. A word that had stopped meaning anything years ago. Her mother's lipstick, the same color as the flower, clung to the rim of her paper cup in a perfect half-moon. The color always reminded her of closing arguments, of her mother's voice in a register just above mercy.

"You were good," her mother added, glancing at her reflection in the window more than at her daughter. "You could be louder, though. Project. It's confidence that people remember." She nodded, her throat tightening around the sound she did not make. She had learned early that silence was safer than correction. "We should go after the second half," her mother said, her tone the same one she used for verdicts. "Parking will be impossible."

Her words landed softly, but underneath them was the familiar rhythm of control disguised as practicality. The way love sometimes arrives as instruction. The poinsettia's red seemed to bloom louder under the fluorescent lights. She studied the flower instead of her mother, tracing the gold veins along its petals, thinking how strange it was that something so bright could grow in winter.

For a moment, she imagined handing it to someone else. To the gray-haired teacher or the janitor sweeping up programs by the door, or even a stranger outside who looked like he needed something beautiful to hold. But she said nothing. She only nodded again and took a sip of her cocoa, the sugar coating her tongue with a sweetness that did not reach her chest. Outside, the night pressed its face against the glass. "We stay for everyone," she said, before she could stop herself. "We clap. That's the whole point."

Lydia's smile tightened, then released, a curtain pulled and let go. "Of course," she said. "Of course, darling." Lydia scanned the room, then, without knowing why. The noise was its own weather; cocoa machines hissing, laughter spilling in uneven waves, chairs scraping across tile, mittens dropped and found again. A microphone squealed somewhere, then cut out. Someone called a name that was not hers, and yet she turned. She never found what she was looking for.

She never knew what she was looking for. Only sometimes, in crowds, she felt a pull deep in her chest. Small, sharp, and untraceable. As if someone, somewhere, had said her name in a language she had not learned yet. For a heartbeat, Lydia thought she saw him. A man near the far door, shoulders slightly hunched, hands in his coat pockets. Miles was not remarkable.

No taller than anyone else, no brighter in the light, but something about the stillness around him drew her eye. He stood apart, quiet in a room that was all sound. He shifted, and a folded program slipped from his pocket. When he bent to pick it up, she noticed a flash of color; something pale and frayed, like a ribbon that had been touched too many times. He did not buy anything.

Did not speak to anyone. Just turned, as if remembering the cold outside, and stepped toward the door. When she blinked, the door was only a door again. Lydia told herself it was nothing. A trick of the lights, a shape mistaken for meaning. She was not the kind of woman who believed in ghosts. But she was the kind who left space for questions. Later, when the second half began, Eleanor sang with a note she did not know she had. It came from somewhere low and certain, somewhere older than her.

The teacher looked up sharply, surprised, then smiled and kept conducting. The music rose and filled the room like a tide. Afterward, she stood in the aisle accepting compliments: *"excellent job, beautiful voice, you are growing up so fast,"* and smiling the right kind of smile, the kind that lands where it is supposed to. But her eyes kept drifting to the lobby doors, to the glass panes reflecting the empty night beyond them.

It felt to Eleanor like the dark was trying to speak, like the wind was spelling something only she could almost understand.

★ ✪ ★

At home, the poinsettia claimed the kitchen table like a red argument. The petals caught the overhead light and reflected it back, too glossy to be trusted.

Her mother had placed it precisely in the center, aligning it with the edge of the saltshaker, the corners of the place mats, as if it were a compass, or a decree, or proof that symmetry could keep chaos away. "Pretty," she said, stepping back to admire it.

Eleanor nodded, but all she could see was the space it assumed, the way it divided the table into two perfect halves. "You were good," her mother had said during dinner that night, slicing leftover chicken with neat, efficient strokes. The knife made a sound like a zipper closing. "You could be great if you learned to smile earlier," she added. "I smiled," Eleanor said.

"Late. It reads like reluctance." Her mother's eyes stayed on the knife. "People don't like reluctance. They want to be liked." Eleanor chewed slowly, even though the chicken had gone dry. "Do you want to be liked?" She asked quietly. Her mother blinked up, mouth open, then laughed, short and bright. "I want to be respected."

"And loved?" Eleanor asked. "That's for children." Lydia pushed the plate toward her. "Eat. You burn through dinner when you sing." She hid half of what she wanted to say under a swallow of water. The glass trembled slightly in her hand, catching the kitchen light in small ripples. Her mother continued on, speaking about schedules, deadlines, plans, but her words slid across the surface of the moment like stones skipping across a lake, never breaking through.

She had learned long ago how to bank her words the way people in old houses learned to bank their fireplaces; keep a slow, safe burn through the night so the morning did not start with a shiver. If she spoke too much, the fire might catch. If she said too little, the room went cold. She lived somewhere between those two dangers; her voice kept low enough not to disturb the peace her mother mistook for harmony. After the kitchen, her room. After the clatter of plates and the small sounds of a house pretending it's calm, there would be quiet, the kind that did not judge or require.

The scratch of a pencil against paper. The whisper of imagination, where questions did not need to be spoken to exist. She ate what was on her plate. She nodded at the correct times. Then she rose, carried her dish to the sink, and turned on the tap. The water came out hot and steady, steaming like a spell she half-remembered from *Harry Potter*, the kind where warmth blooms from a wand and turns a cold room kind again.

She watched the steam rise and twist above the sink, pretending it was magic she could control, that the right word might lift the weight in her chest or make the house forgive its own silence. For a moment, she held her fingers beneath it, letting the heat sting just enough to remind her that feelings were allowed. As she headed to bed, she found glitter from the foil wrapping in her hands. She had washed them twice, but the red still clung faintly to her skin.

In her room, the light was soft and uneven, spilling through the curtains like something too tired to enter fully. She closed the door and reached beneath her pillow for the notebook she kept hidden there. The one with the frayed spine and the bent corners, its pages thick with escape. It was filled with doors. Some were tall and narrow, with knobs shiny from imagined hands.

Others were painted in colors no one had ever named: ochre, storm-gray, sea-glass blue. She drew them in pencil first, then traced them over in ink when she was sure. A few had paint peeling in elegant curls, as if the wood itself were learning to become sea, surrendering to the waves one flake at a time. Others had stars inked in the corners, compass points that glimmered faintly where her pen had pressed too hard. Eleanor did not know why she drew them.

Only that each one felt like a question turned into a shape of a boundary and a promise all at once. Sometimes she imagined that on the other side of one of them, someone was waiting. Not to save her, not even to speak, just to stand with her long enough that silence would feel less like absence and more like understanding.

She drew one more before bed: a small door, half-open, light spilling through. Then she closed the notebook and slid it back beneath her pillow, the paper still warm from her hand. In the margin, she had written: *What if the light is just a hallway on the other side? What if the door is not a barrier but a path?* She turned the page, then wrote a sentence she almost crossed out. *Sometimes I feel like the world is calling my name in a voice I cannot quite place. Does blood have a sound?*

She slept with the notebook open, one corner of the page pressed against her cheek, the ink smudging slightly where her breath found it. The last door she had drawn, a narrow one with light spilling through the crack, waited on the paper like a promise that refused to close. In her dream, the red curtain at the school was not a curtain at all but a mouth vast and breathing, its folds shifting like muscle. It moved as if it wanted to speak, to warn, to welcome.

She hesitated, one hand hovering just before the velvet. The air smelled faintly of dust and chalk and something sweetly metallic, like old coins or memory. Then she walked through it anyway. The fabric brushed her shoulders as she passed, warm and heavy, and the texture reminded her of the poinsettia on the kitchen table, the same red that demanded to be noticed. She stepped into the auditorium, but it was not the one from school. This one was stranger; larger, softer, unreal.

The seats were empty, but she could feel the warmth rising from them, as though someone had just been sitting there moments before, leaving behind the heat of their waiting. Light pooled faintly around her shoes, spreading in slow ripples across the wooden stage. The air was so still that her breath felt like a sound. She took one small step forward, then another, until she stood at the center of the stage. The silence pressed close, not hostile but expectant, like something holding its breath. She opened her mouth and sang. Just one note, pure, uncertain, barely more than a hum.

It floated upward and out, threading through the rafters, into the dark corners where sound goes to decide whether to return. For a long moment, nothing happened. Then the dark began to hum it back. Not echo. Echo only imitates. This was the answer. The sound came from everywhere and nowhere, as if the air itself remembered her voice and wanted her to hear it anew. It was low at first, like the hush of a tide, and then it grew, wrapping around her note until the two sounds met in the middle and became something whole.

She closed her eyes and let the vibration move through her bones, just as the teacher had said. It was the feeling of belonging without knowing where, of being called home by something she could not name. The lights above flickered, and for the briefest moment, she thought she saw a figure in the front row.

A man with his head slightly bowed, hands clasped as if in prayer. The sight did not frighten her. It steadied her. Then the lights dimmed, the warmth faded, and the voice slipped away. When Eleanor woke, the notebook was still open beside her, the door she had drawn half-shadowed by morning light.

A single line of her pencil had darkened in the night, as if something, or someone, had traced it from the other side.

Miles did not return to school that winter. What he practiced was not obsession; it was devotion with boundaries. A quiet covenant between longing and restraint. He told himself that love, at its truest, was not pursuit but presence; the kind that asks for nothing, not even to be seen. He learned the teacher's name from the program he had pretended not to read, tracing the printed letters as if they were coordinates to a world he could only orbit. One evening, under the same kitchen light that had seen him through many years of writing, he folded a small envelope and tucked a few bills inside.

He wrote on the front, in his careful hand: *For the girl in the second row who sings through her bones.* No signature. No return address. He then sealed it and carried it to the post office the next morning, the envelope light in his palm, the way hope sometimes is before it settles. When he slid it through the slot, he felt a strange peace, like setting something back where it belonged. He did not sign it; he did not need to. The universe keeps certain receipts without ink. And as he walked home through the thin winter light, past the bare trees and the storefronts still hung with tired garlands, he realized this was the closest he'd come to prayer in years.

Not asking, not waiting, just giving something small into the world and trusting it would find her.

He kept working more hours in the stockroom, a short run on a construction crew that left his shoulders humming at night, a side job sanding a staircase where the wood had been rubbed to a honey he could not stop touching. He brought the smell of sawdust home like a borrowed season. In the kitchen, he ran his hand along the back of the chair as if it were a rail and found himself whispering lines he had copied from Woolf on a postcard taped to the wall: *"What is the meaning of life? That was all. A simple question: one that tended to close in on one with years…"*

The question had haunted him. The answer had turned out to be simple, too: not a meaning in the sky but a child in a yellow dress laughing at leaves, a girl in black singing through bone, a name he had not been allowed to say aloud and therefore had learned to speak with his life. On her twelfth birthday, he bought a lemon and a bar of dark chocolate. He zested the lemon into the batter like the sun. He melted the chocolate in a pan and drizzled it in loops that looked like handwriting. He set the candle and spoke the words. He listened to how *"Happy"* and *"Birthday"* changed when set beside *"My"* and *"Little"*, a grammar of tenderness he had practiced into fluency.

After the flame stilled, he sat for a while, watching the thin smoke curl upward like a memory that did not know where to go. The wax around the wick had collapsed inward, soft and silver.

The room smelled faintly of sugar and dust. The clock ticked somewhere out of sight; slow, patient, kind. Then he pulled a fresh sheet of paper from the stack and began to write a different kind of letter.

✶ ⊶ ✶

My little star,

I have spent so long telling you the story of my waiting that sometimes I forget there is another story, the one where you live your life without me. I try to imagine it. I want it to be full of small mercies. I hope someone taught you how to make an omelet and not be afraid to fail the first few times.

I hope someone showed you how to put your hair up without snapping the elastic, and that when it broke anyway, they laughed with you instead of sighing. I hope someone has loved you gently but well. The kind of love that listens before it speaks, that holds a door without needing to be thanked.

And if none of that happened, if the years were a long hallway without windows, if the light came only in slivers and the floor creaked with loneliness, then let my first job, when you choose me, be to build the windows. We will start small. One frame at a time.

We will open them together and learn which way the house wants to face the light. We will figure out how morning sounds in our own rooms, how laughter travels down our own halls.

I do not want to make up for the years. I could not. I only want to join the ones that come next.

If the world has ever made you doubt that you are worth staying for, let this be the proof you can touch.

I stayed.

Always,

Dad

✶ ⊶ ✶

Miles set the pen down and read it twice.

The words looked back at him, plain, unguarded, true. For the first time in years, he did not feel like he was writing from absence.

He was writing toward something. The candle's last curl of smoke rose like a thread, and in it, he thought he saw light trying to find its way back. He sealed the envelope slowly, pressing the flap with the flat of his thumb until it stuck. The paper felt warm from his hands, still breathing with the ghost of the words inside. He turned it over once, twice, tracing the edge of the fold as if committing it to memory. He did not put it in the shoe box.

For years, every letter had gone there tucked neatly beside the others like ribs protecting something tender. But this one was different. This one felt alive, restless, unwilling to be stored away. He set it on the table instead, apart from the stack, and looked at it as if it were a bird lighting on a wire. Fragile, temporary, capable of flight if startled. The faintest breath of air might send it elsewhere. He thought: *"Soon."* The words came like a pulse, not a plan. Then, softer: *"Not yet perhaps."* His heart answered both truths at once.

He sat there for a long time, elbows on the table, the room holding its breath around him. Outside, the night deepened, streetlights flickering against the window like signals from another life. He knew he could walk to the post office right now. He could drop it in the blue box, listen to it fall, and let the world decide the rest. But the act felt sacred in its incompleteness. Like faith half-spoken, like the hush before an amen.

He leaned back, eyes on the envelope's pale skin, and whispered to the stillness, *"Not mine to decide."* The words did not feel like surrender. They felt like they could trust. And for the first time in a long time, that was enough. He sat there for a while after, the candle guttering low, the silence gentle instead of sharp.

Trust, he realized, was not a promise that things would come right; it was the quiet courage to stop wrestling the universe. To leave a space open. To let the world move toward you if it ever chooses to. Outside, the city exhaled. The first faint wind of spring brushed against the windows, carrying the scent of thawing earth and the far-off hum of traffic. The rain had stopped, but the street still glistened like a holding breath. That spring, he saw her again without hunting her down.

A flyer for the school's art night was pinned to the corkboard at the coffee shop, curling at the corners from too many hands. It had the same careful typeface as the choir programs, the same polite invitation to the public. Public meant safe. Public meant no one could mistake his presence for trespass. Public meant he could stand at the edge of her world and ask for nothing. He went on a Thursday, after his shift, still smelling faintly of cardboard and dust from the stockroom.

He changed his shirt but not his shoes. He told himself to look like any other man who'd wandered in because he had a niece, or curiosity, or too much time and not enough money. He practiced the expression in the mirror that passed for normal: mild interest, no hunger. The gym smelled of popcorn and varnish.

Poster boards leaned against the walls like shy children, and folding tables held raffle jars, paper crafts, and the kind of baked goods people make when they want to be generous without getting personal. The fluorescent lights made everything look a little too honest. Voices ricocheted off the walls. A basketball bounced once somewhere behind a curtain and then stopped, like someone remembered what the room was for.

He stayed near the back, where the banners hung and the
air was cooler. He did not scan faces the way a desperate
person might. He scanned motion. Hands. Posture. The
small habits that survive new haircuts and growth spurts
and the years he had not been allowed to witness. He
told himself he was here for the drawings. Doors, he
remembered. Doors and light. He told himself he could
leave after one lap.

Then he saw them: a cluster of student tables near the
far wall, each with a sign printed on white card stock.
CHARCOAL. WATERCOLOR. MIXED MEDIA. And
beneath one of them, the word that tightened his throat like
a fist: DOOR STUDIES. He didn't move closer. He didn't
need to. The drawings were visible from where he stood if
he leaned just enough to look like he was reading the raffle
basket descriptions. He read them anyway, because doing a
normal thing was a kind of camouflage.

Doors, mostly. Some painted open. Some stubbornly
shut. One with a narrow slice of light underneath, the line
so thin it was almost an accident. It looked like a promise
trying not to be noticed. Someone laughed quick, bright,
a girl's laugh, but the sound did not land on him until he
heard a name. Not shouted. Not ceremonial. Just said the
way the world says names when it assumes it owns them.
"Eleanor, come look at this one."

The word hit him with quiet force because it belonged to
the room. It belonged to the air. It belonged to people who
could speak it without consequence. He felt the familiar
ache of it: wanting to say it himself, wanting to taste it,
wanting to let it be ordinary. Eleanor lifted her head. It
wasn't dramatic. No music, no spotlight, no slow cinematic
turn. Just a girl rising from a bend over paper, hair falling
forward and then pushed back with the side of her hand.

She looked older than the girl on the stage had looked from the back row. Taller now, in the unmistakable way children become something else when you aren't there to notice the change in increments. Her face held a steadiness that didn't belong to childhood. She smiled at someone off to her left, brief and practiced, then looked back down at the table like the room required her to be composed.

Miles did not step forward. His body did the old thing it had learned: stillness that passes for calm. His hands stayed in his pockets. He focused on her hands instead of her face, because hands were safer to study. Hands didn't accuse. Hands didn't invite you to imagine too much. She picked up a pencil and tapped it twice against the table before making a note on a little index card. Tap, tap. A small ritual. Then she smoothed the edge of a paper with her palm, as if flattening it could flatten whatever she carried inside her.

Her fingers moved before her mouth did when she spoke again, gesturing once, quick, nervous, tender. The gesture pierced him, because it felt familiar in a way he did not have permission to name. He turned his head slightly, pretending to read the label on a tray of brownies. CHOCOLATE WALNUT, $2. He read it twice. He let his breathing match the room's rhythm. He told himself he could leave right now and no one would notice he had ever existed.

A raffle volunteer caught his eye and smiled. "Tickets?" She asked. Buying was normal. Normal meant invisible. He nodded and handed over a few bills. The roll of tickets landed in his hand with a soft paper slap. He didn't want them. He wanted the excuse of them. He tore one off and dropped it into a jar without looking at the prize. A gift basket. A restaurant certificate. A new blender. Hope packaged in cellophane.

He stayed long enough to be believable. Long enough for his presence to become just another adult in a room full of them. Then he pivoted, slow and unremarkable, and moved toward the exit. Halfway there, he saw Eleanor turn again, not toward him, not exactly. Her eyes lifted to the double doors, to the narrow window pane where the night sat behind the glass. For a moment her gaze paused, as if she'd felt something tug in the air. She didn't smile.

She didn't frown. She just looked like a person listening for a sound they can't prove they heard. He stopped breathing for one beat. Then someone spoke to her and the moment broke. Her head dipped. The room swallowed her back into its noise. He pushed the door open and stepped outside into the thin spring air. It smelled like damp asphalt and distant creosote, the city's brief attempt at softness.

The door clicked shut behind him. Not loud. Just final enough. He walked home with the strip of raffle tickets in his pocket like a small lie. Her name stayed in his mouth, bitter and bright, a taste he wasn't allowed to swallow. He did not turn back. He did not reward himself with one more look.

He had learned the rule the hard way: leaving while the door is still open hurts less than waiting for it to close.

For weeks after the concert, Eleanor carried a sense of having almost recognized something and told no one. It was private work, the kind a person does with the door closed and the lamp low. She found herself noticing hands.

The grocery clerks clean nails, the barista's chipped black polish, the principal's square wedding band.

She looked at the way men kept their shoulders, as if
their posture could tell her whether they had learned to
carry something besides themselves. In English class, they
read a piece of nonfiction. The kind of essay that pretends
to be simple but leaves you a little unsteady afterward, as if
something small inside you has shifted without warning.

The teacher, a kind man with chalk dust always on his
sleeves, asked them to write a paragraph using the word
"nevertheless." Eleanor said it like it was her favorite word
in the language, "a hinge word," she called it, "the one that
lets despair open just enough for hope to get a foot in."
She was twelve now, old enough to hear double meanings
and young enough to believe they mattered. She turned
her paper over and stared at the blank side, the blue lines
running across it like quiet instructions.

Around her, pens tapped, pages rustled, and someone
sighed too loudly. The fluorescent lights hummed. Eleanor
could feel the clock ticking behind her shoulder. The word
"nevertheless" pulsed in her mind, stubborn and alive.
Eleanor did not think. She just wrote. *"Nevertheless, love
is not the absence of absence; it is the way a person learns
to stay without being seen."* She stopped. Reread it. The
words felt older than she was, as though someone else had
handed them to her.

Eleanor was not sure what they meant, not really, but
they felt true in a way that truth rarely does when you are
still young enough to be surprised by it. For the rest of the
day, she carried the sentence like a secret. It burned in her
chest and shimmered behind her ribs, equal parts pride and
panic. She worried it might be visible somehow, that people
would look at her and see it written across her skin.

At lunch, she kept her notebook closed.

In history, she doodled over the margin where the sentence might show through the page. In choir, she sang too carefully, afraid that the sound of her voice might give her away. When the teacher handed the papers back the next morning, hers had a small check mark in the corner, nothing more. No underlines. No comments. No sign that he had even paused over the line that had cost her sleep. No one mentioned it. That hurt a little.

And relieved her more. She stared at the faint gray check mark as if it could change meaning under her gaze. It was the kind of mark teachers make when they don't want to touch what they've noticed. She kept the paper flat on her desk until the bell rang, guarding it like it might fly away. Outside the window, sunlight pressed against the glass, sharp and bright. Dust floated in slow spirals through the air like something between ash and gold. In the hallway, the sentence returned on repeat the way a song does when you don't know the lyrics but your brain refuses to stop humming it.

She imagined it written on the inside of her ribs. She imagined it folded and hidden inside the smallest pocket of her backpack, right beside the zipper where her fingers always went when she was nervous. At lunch she didn't open her notebook. In history she wrote too neatly, like neatness could erase the strange heat in her chest. In choir she sang carefully, afraid her voice might betray that she had said something too big on paper.

The teachers taught grammar, formulas, and history that moved too quickly, but in those blue-lined pages, she learned the language of waiting. The architecture of *What If.* When the bell rang, she tucked the notebook beneath her arm and walked home through streets that glimmered with the wet sheen of afternoon sprinklers.

The world moved ordinarily with cars passing, dogs barking behind fences, a boy kicking a can, yet she felt something threaded beneath it all, something humming just below the noise. As she walked, the sentence followed her like a small ghost tugging gently at her sleeve. *"Nevertheless, love is not the absence of absence..."* The words replayed, steady and strange, as if they were not hers at all but something passed down, a message waiting in the marrow. Eleanor could not explain why, but she had the strange, dizzying sense that someone, somewhere, had been waiting for her to write it.

And in that thought, as wild and impossible as it was, she felt less alone. At home that afternoon, she folded the assignment in half, then in half again, until it became a small square that fit in her palm. She slipped it into her notebook between the pages where she drew doors, the paper warming there as if it were alive. The notebook had become her real education. Some doors she drew wide open, light spilling out like mercy. Others she left half-shut because some truths were easier to imagine than to live.

That night, when she opened her notebook again, the folded essay was still there. She touched the crease with her fingertip, tracing it slowly, as if the paper itself might pulse. Then she turned to a blank page, drew another door.

This one tall and narrow, light seeping through from the bottom, and wrote beneath it: *"Some things wait even when we stop looking for them."* One Saturday, she took the bus to the planetarium. The morning was pale and ordinary, but she wanted the kind of quiet that did not ask questions, and the bus offered exactly that. Just the low rumble of its engine and the blur of streets sliding by.

Eleanor sat near the back, watching sunlight stutter through the windows as the city changed from brick to glass to parkway. She had gone once before, long ago. Her mother's idea of a "learning day." It had ended with a migraine, a missed dinner reservation, and a lecture about the cost of tickets and how the stars looked the same from home if you knew where to stand. But she went now for a different reason. The sky, she thought, was the one place where names were agreed upon. It did not matter who you were or what you had lost; Orion was Orion for everyone.

There was comfort in that: a language of light no one could rewrite. She sat beneath the dome and let the dark take her gently, as if it had been waiting for her. The ceiling curved above her like the inside of an enormous palm, and when the lights went out, the air changed; thicker, reverent, full of unseen things. Then, one by one, the stars appeared. They clicked on like switches in a sleeping house. A single voice filled the dark: low, steady, velvet. "That's Lyra… and Vega there, the brightest in the Summer Triangle… and Cygnus, stretching his wings."

The words floated through the air like lullabies, names anchoring light to meaning. She tilted her head back and let them wash over her, until the boundary between her body and the vastness above her blurred. For a moment, she felt exceedingly small, and yet, somehow, very located. As though her place in the pattern, however tiny, had finally been named. When the show ended, no one clapped.

People simply sat there for a moment, dazed, before the lights brightened and reality began to hum again. In the gift shop, she wandered between shelves of constellations printed on mugs and glow-in-the-dark stickers, meteorite fragments in tiny glass boxes.

She picked up a postcard of the night sky painted black, infinite, impersonal, and set it down again. Instead, she chose a thin gold necklace that had a star and a small key-shaped charm dangling from it like a joke the universe didn't explain. The metal looked cheap, but it felt deliberate in her palm, cool and steady, as if it had been waiting in that rack for her to notice. It weighed almost nothing, and yet it carried something she could not name.

Something like a promise. Something like pull. The kind of small, invisible gravity that might one day lead a person home. She paid in cash, slipped the necklace into her pocket, and stepped back into the day's light. The sky outside was pale and empty, but for the first time, she felt it was holding something just for her. Back home, she took the star to her room and held it over her notebook. Eleanor drew a door that was not a rectangle but an arch, softer at the shoulders, less like an argument.
In the margin, she wrote,
"What if keys are not for locks but for courage?"

"Dinner!" Her mother called up the stairs. "Coming!" Eleanor answered, and tucked the gold star into her pocket like contraband hope. At the table, the poinsettia had given up trying to be fierce. Its red had dulled into a tired rust, the once-glossy leaves now browned at the edges; papery, fragile, dignified in their surrender. It sat in the same chipped pot it had come home in, wrapped in crinkled foil that caught the light like old jewelry.

Her mother trimmed the leaves with a small pair of scissors meant for coupons, the kind that lived in a drawer full of pens that did not write and batteries that might still hold a charge. She did it carefully, tenderly, as if the act of tending to something half-dead proved her control over decay itself.

The soft snip of each cut marked time in the room with
a slow, deliberate rhythm that sounded too loud against the
quiet hum of the refrigerator. "Still looks nice," her mother
said without looking up, her tone light and defensive, the
way people speak when they have already had the argument
in their heads. "Just needs a little care." Eleanor nodded.
She did not say that the poinsettia had started to smell
faintly metallic, like old coins and regret.

She did not say that no amount of trimming could bring
the green back, that some things are not meant to bloom
forever indoors. The late afternoon light slanted across the
table, striking the rim of her mother's coffee cup, a lipstick
stain the same red as the poinsettia's dying leaves. The air
carried a faint mix of coffee grounds, bleach, and the ache
of a home that tried too hard to appear fine. Eleanor took
a sip of her water and watched her mother work, the slight
frown of concentration between her brows, the sharpness in
her movements that came from years of fighting everything
she could not name.

The kitchen smelled faintly of lemon cleaner and steam.
That kind of sterile warmth that never quite felt like home.
Rain whispered against the window, gentle but unrelenting,
tracing crooked paths down the glass. The overhead light
hummed. Somewhere in the walls, a pipe ticked. At the
table, the poinsettia had given up trying to be fierce.

Its leaves, once defiant and red, had browned at the
edges, curling inward as if trying to protect what little
color remained. Her mother, Lydia Harper, who never did
anything halfway, trimmed the dead edges with scissors
meant for coupons, her motions careful, controlled, and
without pause. There was love somewhere in this, she
thought; thin, disciplined, and worn to its threads. Love that
trimmed instead of nurtured.

Love that stayed because leaving had already been done once. The scissors clicked again. A leaf drifted softly to the table and curled in on itself, quiet as a sigh. Lydia did not look up when she spoke. "Next month is the middle school meeting. Advanced placement track." Her mouth twitched, not quite humor. "And you'll audition again when they ask. I don't want excuses." Eleanor's throat tightened. "I like singing," she said.

"You like a lot of things." Lydia sighed. The scissors clicked again, sharp and clean. Red leaves fell like used stamps, small and surrendered. "Liking isn't a plan." Her mother said. "It doesn't have to be," She murmured. Lydia didn't hear her or chose not to. "Quiet doesn't suit you lately."

"School," Eleanor said, careful. "School doesn't make you quiet, it makes you tired. Quiet means you are thinking. And thinking, at your age, usually means trouble." Lydia replied, voice firm, cutting through the room the way the scissors cut through stems. "I'm just thinking about next year," Eleanor said. "That's good," Lydia said. "Think forward. Always forward. The past doesn't feed you." Eleanor wanted to say *it can starve you, though*, but she didn't.

The clock above the stove ticked, each second landing heavy. The hum of the refrigerator joined it, steady as breath. When Lydia finally set the scissors down, she noticed the small star hanging from her daughter's zipper, gold, scratched, but gleaming faintly in the kitchen light. Her voice came lightly, but her eyes did not. "What's that?" Eleanor touched it; her fingers were gentle. "A necklace, from the planetarium," she said. "We don't have money for trinkets," Lydia said quickly. "I used birthday money," Eleanor said quietly.

"You should save." Her mom added. "I am." She sighed. Eleanor softened her tone, as if gentleness might earn her space to keep this one small thing. "I just wanted… something to hold." The silence that followed was sharp. Lydia's mouth did that thing again; tight, then smooth, as if she had caught herself before letting an authentic expression escape. "You have everything you need," she said, and her voice was kind. Too kind. The kindness that felt like being told not to ask for air. "Eat." She obeyed. She always did.

She picked up her fork, pressed it into the overcooked chicken, and chewed even though her stomach was already full of things she could not say. Rain began again outside, harder now, beating softly against the glass like fingertips asking to be let in. Her mother poured another cup of tea; black, strong, no sugar. She stirred it even though she never added anything, the spoon clinking against the mug just to give her hands something to do. "Mrs. Ellison said your choir performed well," Lydia said finally, in that measured tone she used when evaluating the air for rebellion. "You had the solo?"

"Yes," Eleanor answered. "You didn't tell me." Her mother responded. "You didn't ask." She said with a smirk. That earned her a look; not angry, exactly, but startled, as though she had forgotten her daughter had teeth. Lydia set the spoon down, aligning it perfectly with the mug's handle. "I ask what matters."

"It mattered to me." She said with some emotion. "Then I'm asking now," Lydia replied "Did you sing it well?" Eleanor hesitated. She wanted to say yes, but the truth was stranger, softer. "I felt it," she said instead. "All of it." For a moment, Lydia's expression faltered, some shadow passing through her eyes too quickly to name.

Then she said, "Feeling is good in moderation. The world rewards discipline." The old conversation, the one they had been having for years, hung between them again. Her art versus her mother's order, her heart versus her mother's armor. Lydia rose and crossed to the sink. The sound of running water filled the room. Steam rose, curling around her hair like smoke. "I know you think I'm hard on you," she said over the sound. "But life is harder. I am preparing you. You'll understand one day."

"I know," Eleanor said, because it was the safest answer. She did not add: "But I do not want to understand if it means becoming you." Lydia rinsed the scissors and dried them with a paper towel. "And don't let that flower die completely," she said, nodding to the poinsettia. "There's no reason something pretty should wither in plain sight." Eleanor glanced at it. The plant was stemmed now, its remaining petals hanging on out of sheer stubbornness. "I'll try," she whispered.

When Lydia left the room, her heels clicked down the hallway in precise rhythm, a sound Eleanor had learned to read like a weather pattern; steady, sharp, warning of storms. Eleanor exhaled. The air left her lungs like surrender. She looked down at the plate. The chicken had gone cold. The poinsettia leaned slightly toward the window, one petal trembling in the draft.

She reached out, gently touched the edge of it, and whispered, "You did your best." Then she looked at the necklace again, the small star catching the light. Keys, she thought, were not always for locks. Sometimes they were reminders that doors existed at all. Her gaze drifted to the window, to the reflection of her own face layered over the darkened street beyond.

The rain ran down in long, shivering threads, and for a moment, she imagined it was a curtain. One she could step through, one that led somewhere she did not have to measure every word she said. Behind her, the sound of her mother's voice floated down the hallway, on the phone now, brisk, professional, all control again. The tone she used with clients and colleagues, not children. She pressed the star against her palm until it left a faint imprint. It hurt just enough to remind her she was real. She thought about her father then, not as a face, but as a possibility.

Someone who might have let the flower die because sometimes things needed to end on their own. Someone who might have said, "Keep singing," instead of, "Liking doesn't pay." The thought was dangerous. So, she held it close, secret, and glowing, like a coal hidden in her chest. Rain continued to fall, steady and patient. She sat there long after her plate was empty, long after the house had gone still. The clock ticked. The refrigerator hummed. The world moved. She stayed.

Somewhere, deep in the quiet between drops, she thought she could almost hear a faint, rhythmic sound beneath the rain, like pen against paper. A sound that belonged to someone who had not stopped writing. That night, the city sighed into rain, the soft kind that seems to remember where it has fallen before.

Eleanor lay in bed with the star necklace turned in her fist. The thin metal pressed its shape into her skin until it hurt just enough to feel real. Rain worked the gutters like a careful harp: steady, deliberate, more prayer than weather. Each drop sounded like punctuation for a thought she hadn't finished. On her nightstand sat her notebook, the one with doors drawn in the margins.

She opened it to a blank page and drew another, quick and instinctive: a door with a sliver of light beneath it. Then, under the drawing, she wrote one sentence, smaller than her homework, smaller than her name: *What if a door is not a barrier but a choice?* She stared at the words until the room blurred. Then she shut the notebook and slid it under her pillow like contraband. When she turned off the lamp, the dark arranged itself gently around her.

Outside, the rain softened. The city exhaled. Two windows held their small squares of light against the dark. And if longing has gravity, if love can bend the air between two lives, then perhaps, for one brief, miraculous breath of the night, the light under his door and the light under hers touched. Neither of them woke with the emptiness they'd carried all week. Only the feeling, faint and impossible, that something somewhere had shifted quietly, without forcing it.

Eleanor slept with the window cracked, because she had learned that air could be a bridge, that wind could travel where words could not.

Miles knew this rain. It was the sound of other beginnings, of streets washed clean and windows lit from within, of moments when the world resets itself without asking permission. He turned off the radio, leaving only the hum of the refrigerator and the whisper of water against glass.

The air smelled of dust and wax and the faint iron scent of weather. Somewhere a siren threaded through the distance, rising, fading, gone.

He sat at the table with the *Year 12* envelope still there, pale against the wood, as if it had its own small heartbeat. He had sealed it hours ago. He had not moved it since. The candle had burned down into a shallow lake of wax, and the wick had folded in on itself like it was tired of being brave. Miles ran his thumb along the envelope's edge. The paper was warm where his hands had held it, still breathing with the ghost of the words inside.

For years, every letter had gone into a shoe box, tucked neatly beside the others like ribs protecting something tender. But this one had refused the box. This one felt alive, restless, unwilling to be stored away. He thought of the blue mailbox a few blocks away. He could walk there right now. He could listen to the envelope drop, the small final sound of surrender. He could let the world decide what happened next. But the act felt sacred in its incompleteness. Like a door left unlatched on purpose. Like faith half-spoken.

Miles watched the envelope the way a man watches a sleeping animal he's afraid to startle. He leaned back, eyes burning, and whispered to the stillness, *"Not mine to decide."* The words didn't feel like surrender. They felt like trust. And for the first time in a long time, that was enough. The candle had long gone to smoke, the letter sealed and waiting like a heartbeat trapped inside an envelope.

He sat at the table long after the wax had cooled, tracing the grain of the wood with the side of his thumb, feeling for the pulse of what he had written. It was strange how words could feel alive, how a few lines of ink could hum faintly against the skin, as if they were already reaching for someone. Outside, the rain had softened into a delicate whisper.

It touched both their roofs; hers, steady and rhythmic against the shingles; his, slower, like breath against old glass, one drop after another, as if tracing a single, invisible line between them. He imagined her asleep, though he could not remember what her room might look like now. Maybe there were books piled on the nightstand, a lamp she forgot to turn off, a cup of tea had gone cold beside something half-written.

He imagined her dreaming of nothing, dreaming of everything. The clock in the kitchen clicked past midnight. He did not blow out the last trace of smoke curling from the candlewick. He let it fade on its own, the air carrying the faint scent of burnt wax and longing. Somewhere, blocks away, not far in miles, but in years, Eleanor turned in her bed, the paper with the word *"Father"* folded beneath her pillow.

The rain pressed softly against her window, tapping a rhythm she almost recognized. For a while, neither slept deeply. It was the kind of night that feels like a hinge on something about to give, though you cannot yet name what. Then, sometime after midnight, when the city had gone entirely too quiet, no sirens, no laughter, no wheels on wet pavement, they dreamed. Each in their own house. Of a door. Not the same door, but the same light beneath it; the slim, steady kind that means someone is awake on the other side. Not waiting to pounce. Not waiting to preach.

Just waiting. Waiting with patience instead of demand, with faith instead of proof. And if dreams have gravity, if longing can bend the air between two lives, then perhaps, for one brief, miraculous breath of the night, the light under his door and the light under hers touched. Neither of them woke with the emptiness they had carried for so long.

Only the feeling, faint, impossible, and holy in its smallness, that someone, somewhere, had finally turned the knob.

Growing in Shadows

Eleanor grew up in a house where silence was louder than words. Not the peaceful kind of silence, not the gentle quiet of early mornings or snowfall before dawn, but the kind that pressed against the ears, dense and watchful, as if listening for any sound it could punish. The walls were white, always white. Repainted every few years with methodical precision, the rollers gliding over old layers as if color itself were a liability.

White didn't argue. White didn't remember. White didn't betray what had once been said too sharply or not said at all. Still, she learned early that no amount of paint could seal what seeped into a house over time. The arguments lingered anyway, faint but persistent, like water stains that reappear after every storm. Furniture sat where it had always sat, arranged for appearance more than comfort. Cushions stayed fluffed. Coasters were never optional.

The television volume remained low enough to be polite, high enough to avoid conversation. Every object had a place, and every place had rules. She learned those rules the way some children learned prayers, by repetition, by consequence, by watching closely. Her mother moved through the house with purpose, heels clicking softly against tile, keys always set in the same bowl by the door. Even rest was efficient. Even affection arrived scheduled and contained, delivered in gestures that looked correct from the outside: a note left on the counter, a reminder about lunch money, a hand briefly resting on her shoulder before pulling away. There were no slammed doors. No shouting matches. No dramatic exits. The quiet was too disciplined for that.

Instead, words were rationed, measured, and released
only when necessary. Questions were answered but rarely
invited. Feelings were acknowledged the way weather is
acknowledged: observed, noted, and then moved past. She
learned to make herself small in that space. Not invisible,
never invisible, but manageable. She learned which
questions earned sighs and which earned nothing at all. She
learned how to swallow disappointment before it appeared
on her face.

She learned that longing could exist without permission,
tucked safely behind the ribs where no one could correct
it. At night, lying in her bed beneath the faint hum of the
house settling, she listened to the silence move. Pipes
clicked. The refrigerator sighed. Somewhere, a clock
counted seconds like a dare. In those moments, she
imagined what sound might fill the rooms if it were allowed
to. Laughter that lingered, footsteps that didn't hesitate, a
voice calling her name not to instruct, but simply to hear it
spoken.

She didn't yet have the language for what was missing.
She only knew that the quiet felt crowded, and that
something in her was always waiting for a noise that never
came. And so she learned to listen harder than anyone else
in the room. Her mother liked the order of white walls, the
way they did not give anything away.

She said it plainly, often, as if explaining a philosophy
instead of a decorating choice. "White keeps things clean,"
she'd say. "White keeps the mind clear." To Eleanor, the
walls looked less like blank canvases and more like pages
someone had already decided not to write on. Pages torn
from a book before the story could begin. The house was
curated with care.

The kind of care that looks generous from the outside and feels restrictive from within. Picture frames lined the hallway at precise intervals, hung level to the millimeter. Her at five, in a school dress too stiff for recess. Her at nine, front teeth missing, smile already learning when to appear and when not to. In another photo, her hair was smoothed flat, her eyes already learning how to hold back. Cousins were laughing around long holiday tables. Aunts with wine glasses tilted just so.

Her mother in tailored jackets at charity luncheons, smiling beside men in suits whose names she never remembered but whose watches always gleamed. The photos told a coherent story: success, stability, respectability. And yet, there was always a missing space. No photographs of her as a baby in anyone's arms. No image of her mother looking tired but happy, bent protectively over a crib. No framed moment of a family of three. Just a clean omission, as deliberate as the white walls themselves.

She noticed early. Children notice absences the way animals sense storms. Once, years earlier, young enough to believe answers might be offered if she asked carefully, she had tried. They were in the laundry room. Her mother stood at the ironing board, pressing a crease into slacks that already seemed sharp enough to cut. The iron moved with controlled force, back and forth, steam rising in short, disciplined bursts. "Where's Dad?" She dared to ask. The question landed badly. She could tell immediately. Her mother didn't look up. She didn't pause long enough to suggest thoughtfulness, just long enough to suggest calculation. The iron hissed. Steam filled the room. The silence stretched tight. "He's gone," her mother said at last. The words were clipped, efficient. Final.

"Gone where?" She pressed, softer now, instinct already telling her she was approaching a boundary. Her mother lifted the iron, set it down with care. Smoothed the fabric with her palm as if the cloth had offended her by wrinkling. "Gone," she repeated. Then, without turning, "Do not think about it." The iron touched cloth again. The hiss returned, louder this time, filling the space where questions might have lived. The rhythm of it was unmistakable, order reasserting itself, heat applied until resistance flattened.

The subject was closed. She stood there, holding a sock she'd meant to match, watching steam curl toward the ceiling and disappear. She didn't ask again. She learned, in that moment, that some questions were not unanswered because they were unimportant, but because they were dangerous. Later, her mother mentioned a meeting with the guidance counselor. Not urgently. Casually. As if discussing weather. "They're starting to keep closer notes," Lydia said, folding her napkin with care. "Placement decisions. Course groupings. These things don't announce themselves. They accumulate."

Eleanor nodded again. She knew the rhythm of this conversation. It wasn't about now. It was about making sure nothing unexpected appeared later. "You don't want to limit yourself before you've begun," her mother added, already stacking dishes. Limit yourself. Eleanor repeated the phrase silently, turning it over. She wondered when wanting something had begun to count as limitation.

She carried her plate to the sink and rinsed it clean, the water running longer than necessary, loud enough to cover the sound of thoughts she didn't yet know how to name. And still, beneath the white walls, beneath the photographs and the rules and the careful living, something waited. A question that never learned how to stop breathing.

By then, she was beginning to learn what questions cost. The lesson wasn't delivered all at once. It arrived gradually, through repetition, through the subtle tightening of her mother's mouth, through conversations that cooled the air in a room the moment curiosity appeared. Asking didn't cause explosions. It caused withdrawal. And withdrawal, she learned, was far more frightening. So she stopped asking. Instead, she began collecting fragments, the way some people collect shells after a tide; small, broken things left behind when the larger body has already retreated.

Once, around Thanksgiving, she overheard something she was never meant to hear. She had been clearing plates, her arms full, the smell of turkey and rosemary thick in the kitchen. She passed behind her aunt, close enough to hear the murmur meant for someone else. "Poor thing," her aunt said, not unkindly. "Looks just like him." She froze for half a second, heart tripping over itself. "Like who?" She almost asked. But her aunt had already turned away, voice lowered, the comment dissolved into clatter and laughter.

She carried the plates to the sink, hands shaking, replaying the words until they felt worn smoothly. Just like him. Whoever he was. Then there was Christmas, she remembered more vividly than the others. Her grandmother pressed a book into her hands, a slim volume of poems, the pages already soft at the edges. She held her fingers a moment longer than necessary, her grip warm and deliberate.

"You always loved reading," her grandmother said as she gave a smile. "Still do." She smiled back. Her grandmother nodded, eyes shining with something like regret. She leaned in, her voice dropping. "Your father loved books, too." The word *Father* sounded different that time. Not sharp.

Not forbidden. Spoken gently, like something that might bruise if mishandled. Before she could respond, her mother appeared, brisk and bright, clapping her hands. "Dessert," she announced. The moment closed like a door pulled shut too quickly. And once, just once, a neighbor slipped. They had been standing by the mailbox, the Arizona sun relentless overhead, she was balancing on the curb while her mother flipped through envelopes.

"Your mom was wild about him in the beginning," the woman said casually, smiling as if she'd shared something harmless. Her mother's head snapped up. "That's enough," she said, voice cool, final. The neighbor flushed. Eleanor stared at the pavement, heat rising to her face, the words *wild about him* echoing like a bell she wasn't allowed to touch. Each moment stayed with her longer than it should have. Too thin to hold. Too fragile to pull on. But impossible to ignore.

She tucked them into the margins of her notebooks, between math problems and song lyrics, written small enough to pass for doodles: *Father, Gone, Loved, Unfortunate thing.* They looked lonely on the page. Like orphans. Like words waiting for their sentence to arrive. Sometimes she tried to imagine him. Not his face. Faces were too easy to invent, too likely to disappoint, but the shape of his absence. The habits he might have left behind without knowing it.

Did he hum when he cooked, off-key and unaware? Did he curse softly when he stubbed his toe, or laugh it off? Did he laugh loudly, filling rooms, or did he smile in a way that warmed the air without making a sound? She wondered if she had inherited anything from him without permission. The way she pressed her knuckle to her mouth when holding back a smile.

The way she lingered over words. The way silence felt
less like emptiness and more like something unfinished.
She thought of him most on her birthdays, especially now,
when they had begun to feel less like milestones and more
like something she hadn't stepped into yet. Every year her
mother gave her a gift, always practical, always useful. A
new coat with reinforced seams. A backpack designed for
"posture support." A set of pens that promised longevity
over beauty.

"You will thank me one day," her mother would say,
arranging the wrapping paper into neat folds. And she
did thank her. She meant it. The gifts kept her warm.
Organized. Prepared. But later, alone in her room, she
would sit on the edge of her bed and feel the quiet
ache arrive, familiar and uninvited. She found herself
wishing, not for something expensive, not even something
permanent, but for something unnecessary. A candle. A
letter. A ribbon tied crookedly, chosen without a reason.
Something that said: *I thought of you not as a responsibility,
but as a miracle.*

She never said this aloud. She learned early that longing,
like questions, was best kept folded small and hidden where
no one could accuse it of taking up space.
Still, it lived in her. Patient. Waiting.

She began to notice how other girls talked about
closeness as if it were something that happened all at once,
a door you stepped through without thinking.

They spoke in half-sentences and shared looks, leaning
toward one another as if secrets had weight. Eleanor
listened more than she spoke, filing the words away without
knowing where they belonged. Sometimes she wondered
if she was standing near something everyone else seemed
to understand. Other times she felt as though she'd been
spared. It wasn't fear that held her back. It was uncertainty.
A sense that whatever people meant when they said like or
crush or love was a language still being taught somewhere
she hadn't reached yet.

She felt it hovering around her, close enough to warm
her hands, not close enough to burn. She paid attention
to moments instead. To the way voices changed when
they said certain names. To the way laughter sharpened
or softened depending on who was listening. To the way
silence could thicken when someone wanted more than they
were supposed to want. She noticed how wanting seemed
to rearrange people, how it made them lean forward or pull
away, how it sometimes made them careless. Eleanor did
not feel careless. She felt watchful.

At night, lying in bed, she tried to imagine what it would
be like to want something without measuring it first. To
reach without rehearsing. The idea made her chest tighten,
not with dread, exactly, but with the strange awareness
that some doors were meant to be approached slowly. That
rushing toward them could mean missing what they were
actually built for.

She did not feel broken. She did not feel behind. She
only felt unfinished. The wanting did not overwhelm her.
Not yet. It lived more quietly than that, settling in small
places between breaths, behind her sternum, in the space
that opened whenever she heard someone say the word dad
without thinking. It wasn't pain. Pain demanded attention.

This was something else. A pressure, mild but constant, like weather you adapt to without realizing you've changed the way you walk. She learned how to move around it. How to keep her voice steady when teachers mentioned family projects. How to listen when friends complained about parents with the careless confidence of people who knew they would be answered. She did not resent them. She studied them. The way one studies a language before knowing how to speak it.

At night, she sometimes pressed her hand flat against her chest, feeling the quiet insistence there, not asking it to leave, only to stay still long enough for her to sleep. And somehow, it left her uneasy. It left her unsure of the word love. Her mother had said it once, in passing, while watching a movie where someone cried too much for someone else. "Love is for children," her mother had said, folding laundry with sharp efficiency. "Adults know better."

Eleanor had nodded then, because nodding was easier than arguing. But lying in the dark now, she turned the sentence over in her mind. If love was for children, then what did that make her? Too old to want it? Too young to understand it? Or simply foolish for hoping it might be real? That year, Eleanor became careful about what she carried with her.

Not in the way her mother meant when she reminded her to pack lunches and spare hair ties, but in the quieter sense, what stayed close to her body, what lived in pockets and margins and folds. She began keeping loose papers tucked inside her backpack instead of in binders. Pages torn from old notebooks. Half-written sentences. Drawings she didn't want graded or explained.

She liked the way they shifted when she walked, the faint whisper of paper reminding her that something unfinished was moving with her through the day. At home, she rearranged her room in small, unnoticed ways. A stack of books migrated from the shelf to beneath the bed. A pencil cup appeared on the nightstand without announcement. Her mother did not comment; these were changes too minor to correct. Eleanor learned early that subtlety was its own permission.

She started writing at night, when the house had settled into its disciplined quiet. Not assignments. Not lists. Just words that arrived without asking to be justified. Sometimes they were sentences. Sometimes they were only fragments. She did not try to make them behave. She let them exist the way thoughts do before they decide what they are. Drawing came first. Doors, always doors. Some she sketched carefully, measuring the proportions with the side of her thumb. Others appeared quickly, almost accidentally, their lines uneven and urgent.

She liked those best. They felt closer to truth. She didn't yet know why she was saving these pages, only that throwing them away felt wrong. She searched in ways that did not require courage yet. On the internet, late at night, with the volume turned low and the glow of the screen dimmed until it felt secret. She typed names, then erased them. Clicked on results, then backed away before the page fully loaded.

There were directories that listed addresses without stories. Old school newsletters archived online, their photos grainy and unhelpful. Mentions of people who might have been him, might not. Sometimes she stopped not because she was finished, but because she felt the edge of something she wasn't ready to touch.

The searching didn't give her answers. But it gave her something to hold on to, something to keep the questions from scattering everywhere at once. So she kept them. Folded. Hidden. Close.

And each night, when she slid them back into place, she felt the small, steady comfort of having made room for something unnamed.

Eleanor excelled in school because it was the only battlefield where her victories were her own. Grades were clean things. Honest. You studied, you earned, you were measured by numbers that didn't care who waited for you at home or who didn't. Straight A's lined her report card like proof she could point to if anyone ever asked why she took up so little space. Her teachers liked her. "Reliable", they said. "Focused".

The kind of student who turned things in early and never caused trouble. She joined the choir because her voice felt truer than her silence, the debate club because arguing within rules felt safer than arguing at home, and the art club because drawing doors had given her a language no one else seemed to speak.

Her mother came to awards nights in tailored jackets and low heels that clicked purposefully across gym floors. She clapped when her name was called. Smiled for photos. Straightened her collar before letting go.

"Good," Lydia would say afterward, slipping the program into her purse. "This will matter later." She asked once, carefully. "Did you hear the solo? In the second song."

"Yes," her mother replied, already unlocking the car. "You were fine. But the advanced track matters. One note doesn't build a future." She learned then how to tuck her wanting away. How to accept praise that skimmed the surface and never ask for the kind that stayed. She wasn't striving for medals. She didn't care about the ribbons curling on her bedroom wall or the certificates stacked neatly in a folder. Those were artifacts, not answers.

What she was searching for was proof; quiet, undeniable proof that she belonged to a story bigger than discipline and achievement. A story where someone noticed not just what she did, but who she was when no one was watching. Sometimes, in dreams, she felt it tug again. Not a face. Not a voice. Just a sensation, warm and sudden, as if someone had thought of her at the exact same moment she'd turned in her sleep. In those dreams, she wasn't alone. She was remembered, she thought, not as a fact, but as a feeling.

She would wake with her heart racing, fingers twisted in the bed sheet, breath shallow with the certainty that love could stretch across miles if you let it. That it could exist without permission. That it could survive being unnamed. But daylight always came. Her mother's words wrapped tight around the morning like plastic around leftovers: "Gone. Do not think about it." So Eleanor didn't speak it aloud. She didn't ask again. She didn't say the word *father* in mirrors or prayers.

She didn't let it slip during late-night conversations with friends or whispered secrets at sleepovers. But she thought about it every day. In hallways crowded with lockers and laughter. In classrooms where fathers volunteered for career days. In the quiet moments when applause faded and she stood alone with her achievements, wondering who they were meant for.

Silence had taught her how to survive.
Longing taught her how to hope.

Around the same time, Eleanor began to understand that some things could be true without being spoken. It started with small rules she made for herself. Nothing dramatic. Nothing anyone else would notice. She decided which questions were safe to ask and which ones stayed folded away. She learned how to nod at the right moments. How to smile without inviting follow-up. Her mother approved of this phase. "You're getting more mature," she said once, adjusting Eleanor's collar before a school event.

The word mature felt heavy, like a coat meant for someone else. Eleanor accepted it anyway. At school, adults praised her reliability. "You're so composed," they said. "So steady." She wondered if steadiness was something you chose or something that happened when you learned what not to disturb. She watched other kids test boundaries loudly. Slam doors. Argue. Cry in public.

Eleanor didn't envy them exactly. She studied them, the way one studies weather patterns from indoors. In her notebook, she began writing shorter sentences. Less explanation. More space between lines. She liked the way white space held meaning without insisting on it.

A sentence didn't need to explain itself to be real. Sometimes she wrote questions and didn't answer them. She drew doors without deciding whether they opened inward or out. She liked leaving them unresolved. It felt honest. She was still a child. She knew that.

She liked cartoons and warm drinks and sitting cross-legged on the floor to do homework. But there was also a part of her that felt older than her years; not wiser, just more alert. As if she were waiting for something she couldn't yet recognize. At night, when the house quieted into its familiar shape, Eleanor would press her palm flat against her chest and feel her heartbeat. Steady. Present. Proof that she was still here, still moving forward even when nothing seemed to be changing.

She didn't know what was ahead. She didn't need to. For now, it was enough to keep space open. She didn't know what would happen next. But for the first time, the distance between wanting and knowing felt different, not smaller exactly, but marked. As if it could be measured one day, even if she didn't yet have the tools. The idea settled into her quietly. Not a promise. Not a plan. Just a recognition. Something had shifted. And whatever lay ahead no longer felt infinite.

It felt paused, attentive, waiting for her to decide when she would understand what moving meant.

Longing Without a Name

Eleanor had never said the word *Father* aloud in her house, but the word lived in her mind like a secret room she kept unlocking. Sometimes the key turned easily, the door opening on its hinges without complaint. Other times it stuck, swollen with silence and years, as if the wood itself had absorbed every unasked question and grown heavy from it. Still, she always went back to the thought of him. To the outline of someone, her heart seemed to recognize, even though her memory could not supply a face. It was a strange thing to miss someone you could not remember. To feel a shape in your life where something essential should have been, like a shadow cast by an object just out of sight.

At school, in the computer lab, she had typed his name once before. Not because she knew it with certainty. She didn't. She only had what her grandmother had let slip one Christmas afternoon, when the house smelled of pine, overcooked ham and old regrets. They had been sitting at the table, passing dishes, when her grandmother paused with the serving spoon hovering midair.

"You have his eyes," she had said softly, almost to herself. Eleanor had looked up. "Whose?" There had been a flicker then of fear, perhaps, or something like remorse. Her grandmother's voice dropped and turned fragile. "Your father's." The room had gone very still.

"Miles Bennett," her grandmother had added, the name escaping her lips before she could gather it back again. She said it like a prayer she hadn't meant to speak aloud. The words fell into the air and broke it open, delicate as glass. Then her grandmother had gone quiet, fussing suddenly with her napkin, folding it and unfolding it as if she could smooth the past flat. She had pretended not to notice.

She'd looked down at her plate, speared a green bean she didn't want. But the name had already taken root, settling somewhere deep and alive. Now, weeks later, under the humming fluorescent lights of the school computer lab, she finally dared to summon it again. The room glowed pale blue from the screens, rows of students haloed by digital light. The air smelled faintly of dust, metal, and pencil shavings ground into the floor by decades of restless feet.

Somewhere, a printer coughed to life. Outside, a steady wind rattled the windowpanes, making the blinds clatter softly, unevenly, like a heartbeat out of rhythm. She sat towards the back, where no one could easily see her screen. Her navy notebook lay closed beside the keyboard, doors hidden inside it like held breath. She placed her fingers on the keys. For a moment, she did nothing.

Then she typed: **Miles Bennett**. The letters appeared slowly, as if her hands did not fully trust what they were doing. Her pulse thudded in her ears. She swallowed. On impulse, brave or reckless, she couldn't tell, she added her own name beside his. **Eleanor Bennett**. The two names sat next to each other on the screen, strange and right at the same time, like two notes that had been waiting for the same chord. Her chest tightened. The cursor blinked. She hit Enter.

For a second, the page went white. Not empty, *Infinite.* The kind of blank that makes you aware of how much you are about to ask of the world. Then the browser filled with fragments. Names. Headlines. Addresses half-buried in directories. Pieces of other people's lives tangled together in the web's endless sprawl. She leaned closer, her reflection faint in the glass of the screen, her eyes doubled over the results, searching themselves as much as the page.

There were too many Bennetts. Too many Miles. Each name a door. Each link a life that was not hers. Her heart knocked hard against her ribs as she scrolled. A mechanic in Denver. A novelist in Portland. A veteran in Ohio. One result stopped her breath short, an obituary photo, the man's face too old, too lined, not the age her father would be now. Relief and grief arrived together, tangled so tightly she couldn't tell which was heavier.

She kept scrolling. And then she saw it. Small. Unassuming. Halfway down the page, almost easy to miss. **Miles D. Bennett ~ SIERRA MESA, AZ**. Her city. No photograph. No story. Just a name and an outdated listing, the kind of digital footprint left by someone who had lived quietly, who had not tried to be found. Her hand hovered over the mouse. She didn't click. She couldn't. It felt as if touching that name would tilt her entire life off its axis.

As if the moment she crossed that invisible line, there would be no returning to the careful, controlled version of herself she had built. Instead, she stared. The cursor blinked beside the address like a tiny, rhythmic breath. She whispered the name once, barely audible. *"Miles Bennett."* The syllables trembled in her mouth, familiar in a way she could not explain, like a word she had known before she knew language.

The name expanded inside her, quiet and enormous. It wanted to become a constellation, something that had always been there, waiting for the dark to clear. The bell rang. The room burst into motion with chairs scraping, backpacks zipping, laughter ricocheting off tile. Someone groaned about homework. Someone else called her name, waved. Eleanor did not move.

She stared at the screen until it dimmed, her reflection growing stronger as the page faded. A girl looking at herself through someone else's ghost. Finally, she shut the monitor off. The screen went black, leaving her face doubled in its glass with eyes full of questions that had waited nearly fourteen years to be asked. She stood, slung her bag over her shoulder, and walked out into the hall. The wind pushed against the school doors as she exited, cold and alive, carrying the scent of rain and dust.

The sky was restless, clouds sliding past one another like thoughts that refused to settle. It felt like the city itself was exhaling. She had language for it by then. She simply avoided using it. Outside, the clouds were moving fast. A storm gathering or clearing. She could not tell. But for the first time, *Father* did not feel like a forbidden word. It felt like direction. And even as she told herself to be careful, even as she tried to tuck the hunger back where it belonged, she knew one thing with aching clarity:

She had already opened the door.

Eleanor began to write him in her notebook, not letters, exactly, but questions released into the air as paper boats set on a river with no visible shore. She didn't address them the way letters are meant to be addressed. There was no "Dear" and no name at the top, because names made things real, and she was not yet brave enough for that.

Instead, the questions simply appeared, as if they had always been waiting for ink. *Do you hum when you cook? What is your favorite season? Did you ever imagine me at fourteen? Do you think I would prefer blue to green? Do you know that I am real?*

They spilled into the margins of her life. Between algebra equations she half-understood and song lyrics she knew by heart. In the blank spaces of test prep booklets. Along the edges of programs from choir concerts. She wrote them small, careful, as if she were afraid someone might overhear her thinking. When she ran out of room, she improvised. Ballpoint pen on the back of grocery receipts. Mechanical pencil on her wrist, later washed away in the sink. Lipstick on a napkin in a diner bathroom when the questions came too fast and paper was nowhere to be found.

Each one felt urgent. Necessary. As if not writing them might cause something inside her to fray beyond repair. None of the questions had answers. That was the hardest part. But writing them down kept her from unraveling. It gave the longing somewhere to sit instead of pacing her chest. It turned the ache into shape. Into language. Sometimes, late at night, she would read them back to herself, her voice barely more than breath.

Sometimes she would stop midway, the words blurring as tears pressed close, and she would close the notebook gently, like shutting a door on a room she loved but couldn't yet enter. Other times, she folded the page in half. Once. Then again. As if the crease itself might become a path. As if folding could make distance smaller. As if paper knew how to travel where she could not.

She would hold the folded page in her palm and think, not aloud, but with the quiet intensity of belief: *Here.* And then, softer: *Catch.* She didn't know if anyone ever did. But she knew this: the questions were real because *she* was real. And somewhere, beyond her seeing, the act of asking felt like a kind of courage. Like standing at the edge of a door, hand raised, trusting that one day it might open.

Her mother noticed the growing quiet the way some people notice a crack in porcelain, by the way it catches the light once you know where to look. "You're distracted," Lydia said one evening, setting dinner plates on the table with the neat, practiced precision of someone who believed disorder invited catastrophe. Forks aligned. Napkins squared. Nothing accidental. Eleanor looked at the plate in front of her, chicken cut thin and even, vegetables arranged as if they were waiting to be judged.

She took a breath before answering, careful not to let it sound like resistance. "I'm fine," she said. Lydia didn't sit. She remained standing, hands resting lightly on the back of Eleanor's chair. That posture, hovering, contained had always meant something was about to be corrected. "This is when habits set," her mother said. "Middle school becomes high school faster than you think. This is when people start falling behind without realizing it."

The words were delivered calmly, as if they were facts rather than warnings. Lydia reached for her fork, then paused. "Focus on your classes. On staying ahead. On keeping your options clean." Options. The word landed with familiar weight. Eleanor nodded. She had learned that nod well, small, agreeable, just enough to signal understanding without surrendering the inside of herself.

"I am focused," she said quietly. Lydia studied her for a moment longer, then seemed satisfied. She sat, began eating, and the conversation moved on to schedules, to placement tests, to which electives would "matter later." Eleanor ate. She chewed. She swallowed. But something in her had already stepped back from the table, retreating to a place her mother could not audit.

Later that night, after the house had gone still and the walls returned to their familiar white silence, Eleanor closed her bedroom door and leaned her forehead against it. She stood there for a long moment, listening to her own breath, to the low hum of the refrigerator down the hall, to the distant sound of traffic moving through a city that never paused long enough to notice who was missing. She crossed the room and sat on her bed.

The navy notebook lay open where she'd left it. Questions crowded the page, written in different inks, different moods. Her backpack rested nearby, the gold star necklace catching the light as if it were trying to speak. She picked it up. The metal was cool at first, then warmed quickly in her palm. Eleanor closed her fingers around it, feeling the familiar edges, the quiet reassurance of something chosen for no reason except wanting it.

She leaned back against the pillows and whispered into the dark, her voice steady now, certain. "You are not the rest," she said. The words felt true the moment they left her mouth. "You are the center." The room did not answer, but it didn't need to. For the first time, Eleanor understood something with aching clarity: some truths do not require permission.

Some loves do not exist to be managed or postponed or explained away. Some doors, once found, refuse to disappear. And no matter how tightly the world tried to narrow her life into plans and bullet points, Eleanor knew this, deep in the place her mother could never reach: She was no longer drifting. She was moving toward something that had been waiting for her all along.

$$\star \; \bullet \; \star$$

In art club, she painted a canvas of a door standing in the middle of a field. Around it grew sunflowers, bright as flares, but the door was slightly ajar, and nothing was visible inside. Her teacher, Mr. Stewart, a gentle man with paint on his knuckles, asked, "Where does it lead?" Eleanor did not answer at first. Eleanor touched the bristles of her brush to clean water and watched the color cloud out. Finally: "Home."

"Home's a good place to paint toward," he said, and moved on. But she knew home was the one thing the painting was not. It was what she wanted beyond the door. Eleanor's friends did not notice the shadows. To them, she was steady. The kind of girl who remembered things when other people forgot. Birthdays. Locker combinations. Deadlines. The exact way someone took their coffee from the vending machine when midterms hit, and everyone was a little too fragile to risk getting it wrong.

She carried extra pencils in her backpack, sharpened and aligned. Spare hair ties looped neatly around her wrist. Band-Aids folded flat in her wallet like emergency promises. When someone scraped a knee, lost a pen, or panicked five minutes before a quiz, Eleanor was already reaching into her bag. "Oh my God, how do you always have one?" Leah would laugh. Eleanor would shrug. "Habit."

She was the quiet heartbeat of their small circle, the one who kept things moving smoothly while the louder ones made the noise of living. She listened more than she spoke. When she did speak, it was usually to steady things. "It's fine," she'd say. "You did great, we'll figure it out." "Here, use mine."

108

She laughed at their jokes, though her laughter often came a second too late, as if she needed to check whether it was safe first. She went to football games and clapped when everyone else clapped, her breath frosting the night air as the cheerleaders' pom-poms caught the stadium lights and exploded into color. She sat cross-legged on bleachers painted in flaking blue, sipping cocoa that scalded her tongue, nodding when someone pointed out who had fumbled or scored.

"Did you see that?" Someone would shout. "Yeah," Eleanor would say, smiling. "Crazy." To them, she was there. Always there. Resolute. Present. Reliable. They did not see how her smile faltered when fathers arrived in pickup trucks after practice with engines rumbling low, headlights washing across the parking lot in warm, forgiving light. They didn't notice how her gaze lingered as doors opened and dads leaned across seats to tease their daughters, to toss jackets over shoulders, to ask if anyone wanted burgers on the way home.

She watched those gestures the way some people watch sunsets, knowing they would end, but unable to look away while they lasted. They did not see how her eyes followed the fathers without her meaning them to, tracing their silhouettes as they backed out of parking spaces and turned down side streets toward lives she could only imagine.

How she memorized the way their laughter sounded, deep, unguarded, carried from the chest instead of the throat. Sometimes someone would say, "My dad's here," with casual relief. Eleanor would nod. "Cool." No one noticed the way she rubbed her thumb against her wrist when the noise grew too loud, or how her shoulders tightened when a man raised his voice, even in laughter.

She had learned the choreography of belonging by heart: how to walk beside friends without seeming apart from them, how to speak without saying too much, how to fill the space left open by absence without drawing attention to its shape. In photographs, she looked radiant enough. The lighting helped. The crowd helped. No one could see that her smile was always slightly off-center, a fraction of hesitation hidden behind her teeth. No one could tell how much effort it took to hold it there.

Sometimes, when a friend's father waved at her, friendly, casual, she would lift her hand too. The gesture always caught in her chest before it reached her fingers, like a word swallowed mid-syllable. She told herself it didn't matter, that she was fine. That everyone had empty rooms inside them. But every so often, when the night grew too still, and her friends' laughter had gone to sleep, she would sit on the edge of her bed with the star-shaped necklace pressed into her palm and feel the echo of something pressing softly against her ribs. Not grief. Not jealousy.

Something quieter. Older. A longing that felt inherited rather than learned. She did not hate those fathers. She envied their ease. The way they carried love without apology. The way they didn't have to wonder if their children thought of them. The way their presence didn't need to be earned or explained, it simply was. The next day, she would wake early, braid her hair tight, and return to the rhythm the world expected.

She would pack her books, meet her friends, and hold the door open for them with a practiced smile. "Thanks," someone would say. "Anytime," Eleanor would reply. And no one, not one of them, would know that she had stayed up half the night wondering what his voice might sound like when he said her name.

Once, at Leah's house, she watched Leah's father carry in a tray of cookies with exaggerated effort, pretending the plate was heavier than it was. "Oh no, I may not survive this journey." He groaned theatrically. "Dad, stop," Leah said, rolling her eyes, but she laughed anyway, loud and unguarded. Eleanor laughed too, because that was what you did. But she watched the laughter more than the cookies.

Watched the way Leah leaned into her father without thinking, the way his hand landed automatically on her shoulder, the way love moved between them like muscle memory. Eleanor felt the truth land quietly and completely. *That is the shape of what I am missing.* That night, she opened her notebook and wrote carefully, deliberately, as if naming it might keep it from hurting more than it already did: *"Absence has a sound. It is the way laughter echoes when one note is missing."*

She closed the notebook and held it to her chest, breathing through the ache, not because it would go away, but because it deserved to be carried with care. The longing did not arrive all at once. It gathered. Quietly. Incrementally. At this age, it felt less like an ache and more like pressure, something present but contained, like air held behind glass. Eleanor learned how to move with it without letting it announce itself. She carried it through hallways and classrooms, through conversations that skimmed the surface of her life without ever dipping below.

It did not interrupt her days. It accompanied them. Sat beside her during lunch. Followed her home. Waited patiently while she slept. She did not tell anyone about it. Not Leah, who noticed most things but not this. Not her teachers, who praised her focus and mistook silence for discipline. And certainly not her mother, who had trained herself never to look directly at unfinished things.

Instead, Eleanor practiced containment. She learned how to hold questions without demanding answers, how to let curiosity exist without converting it into action. Wanting, she realized, did not have to mean reaching. Sometimes it meant standing still long enough to understand what the wanting was asking for. She searched in quieter ways now. Safer ones. The kind that could be closed quickly if footsteps passed her door.

Late at night, with her homework pushed aside and the house sunk into its disciplined hush, Eleanor sat cross-legged on her bed and opened her phone with the brightness turned low enough to feel secret. She typed his name slowly, deleting it once before forcing herself to try again. Search results bloomed and blurred, addresses without stories, names without context, fragments that felt close enough to touch and yet unreachable.

She clicked through public directories she barely understood, school newsletters archived online, scanned yearbook pages from decades earlier where faces stared back without recognition. Sometimes she used the school database meant for research projects, pretending it was for history homework if anyone ever asked. Sometimes she didn't search at all. She just stared at the cursor, blinking patiently, waiting for her to decide what kind of wanting she was allowed.

At dinner, she practiced careful curiosity. "Do you think people change much after high school?" She asked once, pushing peas into a neat line. Her grandmother paused, fork hovering. "Some do," she said slowly. "Some become exactly who they were trying not to be." Another night: "What was Mom like when she was younger?" Her grandmother smiled, soft and brief.

"Very sure of herself," she said. "Very in love." "With…
law?" Eleanor offered lightly. The laugh that followed
didn't quite land. "With a lot of things," her grandmother
said, and reached for her water, steering the conversation
gently back toward safer ground. Eleanor learned when
to stop. When to listen instead of asking. When to store
a sentence away for later. The searching didn't give her
answers.

But it gave the questions somewhere to live without
rattling loose. Eleanor would dream of a man seated at
a small table, lamplight pooling over his shoulders. His
head bent. His hand moving steadily across a page. The
scratch of a pen against paper filled the room, not frantic,
not hurried, but deliberate. Devotional. A candle flickered
nearby, its flame breathing, alive.

She never saw his face. Not once. It was always just out
of reach, turned slightly away, hidden by shadow or angle.
But she felt him, his concentration, his patience, the way his
whole body seemed to lean toward the act of writing as if it
were keeping him upright. As if writing were the thing that
made him real. When she woke, the dream did not fade the
way dreams usually do.

The image dissolved, but the sound remained, the steady
scratch of pen, the quiet persistence of it, lingering in her
ears like a second heartbeat. Eleanor would lie there in the
half-light, hand pressed to her chest, listening. And she
would think, not with certainty, but with something just as
powerful: *Someone is trying to reach me.*

Even if she didn't yet know how to answer.

★ ☉ ★

One evening in early spring, when the world outside her window smelled faintly of wet earth and lilac, Eleanor could not sleep. The air was warm for the first time in months; soft, forgiving, and she had cracked the window open before bed, letting the night drift in. The curtains lifted and fell with each passing breath of wind, slow and patient, as if the house itself were alive and resting. Somewhere down the block, sprinklers ticked on and off. A dog barked once and then reconsidered.

The moon hung low over the neighborhood, pale gold and heavy, wrapped in a thin gauze of cloud that made it look bruised rather than bright. A train sounded in the distance. Its whistle cut through the night: long, lonely, unmistakable. It was the kind of sound that carried history in it, that reminded you how many people had waited for something while listening to that same note stretch across the dark. Eleanor rolled onto her side, then onto her back, then onto her side again.

Sleep refused her. On her nightstand lay the list she had written that morning, the ink already smudged where her palm had rested: *High school orientation, Placement review, Choir rehearsal*. The words looked orderly. Responsible. But tonight they felt strangely misaligned, as if her life had been written in the wrong order, like a story that had skipped its first chapter and was pretending not to notice.

Her gaze drifted to the edge of the bed, to the place where her pillow dipped slightly, and she thought of the word she had folded beneath it weeks ago. *Father*. Unspoken, the word had grown heavier. More insistent. It no longer felt like a question; it felt like a presence.

114

A small, steady light blinking behind her ribs, asking
not for permission, but for acknowledgment. Her chest
tightened. After a moment, she reached beneath the pillow
and pulled out her navy notebook. It was warm from sleep,
its corners softened from years of being carried everywhere.
The pages rippled faintly when she opened it, warped by
ink and time and nights when she had pressed too hard with
the pencil because she needed the words to stay.

She expected the familiar: doors drawn in every
imaginable shape, half-written sentences, stars sketched in
margins when her thoughts outran her courage. But what
she found stopped her breath mid-drift. Near the center of
the notebook, on a page she would have sworn had been
blank, was a single sentence. Not carefully placed. Not
aligned with any margin. It sat slightly crooked, as though
it had arrived without asking her first. Written in her own
unmistakable handwriting:

If you wish, the door is open.

The graphite was paler than the surrounding pages.
Smudged at the edges. Older. As if it had been waiting there
a long time to be found. Her breath caught so sharply it
hurt. The room seemed to contract around her, the silence
tightening, attentive. Even the train whistle had faded,
leaving only the quiet hum of electricity in the walls and the
faint rustle of the curtain breathing beside her.

Eleanor's hand trembled as she traced the sentence with
her fingertip, following each letter slowly, deliberately,
the way one reads Braille, seeking meaning through touch
when sight alone is not enough. The pencil pressure had
indented the page beneath the words. Whoever had written
it, herself, or something through her, had meant it to last.

"I didn't write this," she whispered. The admission made her pulse spike. She searched her memory: nights spent sketching doors, afternoons scribbling thoughts between homework problems, moments of distraction when words had poured out without conscious intent. Nothing. She did not remember writing it. But she did not erase it either. She stared at the line until it blurred, then lifted her eyes to the window.

The curtain stirred again, letting in a cooler draft that smelled faintly of rain. Streetlights shimmered against the glass, each reflection a small rectangle of light with tiny doors opening and closing with the movement of her breath. Her heart hammered. She read the words aloud, testing them in the air. *"If you wish, the door is open."* They did not sound like hers. They sounded borrowed. Returned. Like something spoken once to her and carried back across time.

For a long moment, she simply sat there, the moonlight laying silver bars across her blanket, the sentence glowing faintly under the lamp as if it were alive. As if it had weight. Intention. The logical part of her, the part trained by essays and deadlines and her mother's certainty, scrambled for explanations. She must have written it months ago and forgotten. It came from a dream. It was coincidence.

But another part of her, deeper and older, knew better. The same part that made her search for shapes in constellations. The part that tightened when she heard certain songs. The part that whispered a name she had never been allowed to say. Warmth spread through her chest, not fear, not panic, but recognition. Like the feeling of stepping into a room you didn't know you'd been missing and realizing the furniture remembers you.

As if someone, somewhere, had opened a door just wide enough for light to slip through. Eleanor pressed her thumb to the final word; *Open,* and felt her mouth curve into a fragile, unfamiliar smile. *"Okay,"* she whispered to the quiet, her voice barely louder than the turning of the page. *"Then maybe I'll walk through."* The words hovered there, suspended between breath and belief. Outside, the wind shifted. The curtain lifted higher this time.

The air changed subtly, unmistakably, the way it does when two moments overlap in the same breath. She didn't know what would happen next. But for the first time, the distance between wanting and knowing felt different, not smaller exactly, but marked. As if it could be measured one day, even if she didn't yet have the tools. The idea settled into her quietly. Not a promise. Not a plan. Just a recognition. Something had shifted. And whatever lay ahead no longer felt infinite. It felt paused.

Attentive. Waiting.

A single breath away.

The Mother's Silence

The kitchen was a place of knives. Not only the ones that gleamed in their block by the sink; steel catching slivers of light like secrets waiting to be spoken, but the invisible kind: the sharp edges of tone, the delicate, deliberate cuts made by words said too calmly, and the deeper wounds carved by what was never said at all.

Every surface carried memory. The counter, smooth in places and nicked in others, had listened to years of arguments disguised as dinner talk. The refrigerator hummed like a nervous witness, loyal and relentless. Even the air seemed careful, with the faint tang of lemon cleaner, the slow tick of the clock over the doorway, the steady drip of the faucet where the seal had worn thin, each sound insisting on order, on time, on control.

Eleanor learned early how to move in this room like someone crossing a field of glass; quietly, deliberately, each step a negotiation. She knew when to rattle dishes to fill the silence and when to let the scrape of a chair serve as punctuation. She could sense her mother's mood by the rhythm of the chopping knife alone, quick, controlled, too even. Precision without mercy.

The knives themselves were immaculate, lined in their wooden block with the precision of soldiers. Her mother cleaned them after every meal, even when they hadn't been used, the steel flashing under the tap as though order itself could be polished into peace. Sometimes, when her mother's back was turned, Eleanor stared at her reflection warped in the metal. Her face stretched thin, eyes too large, lips pressed into a line that looked older than her years.

She would hold her breath until the image steadied, until she could tell herself she still belonged to the shape of the room. There were nights when the tension in that kitchen could have been cut with the very knives meant for bread. Her mother's voice, careful, clipped, would ask questions that were not really questions. "Did you finish studying?" First question. "Yes." She answered. "Have you heard from your grandmother?" She added.

"Not today." She responded. "Do you plan to keep that door open all night?" She continued. "I'll close it." She sighed. Each answer was placed gently, like glassware on a shelf that might already be cracked. Eleanor watched the way the stove light caught the faint fractures in the linoleum, the tiny imperfections that made the room feel both lived-in and trapped.

The kitchen table, with its scratches and heat rings, was the safest island in that space, though even there, conversation sometimes drew blood. There were moments when her mother's eyes, sharp and weary, lingered on her too long, as if searching for something she had misplaced years ago. Eleanor would smile. She would keep her voice light. She would make herself small enough to pass inspection. Inside, she could feel the cut, clean, invisible, and deep.

And yet, sometimes, when her mother was not looking, she would notice how the knives glinted just so, reflecting the morning light like stars caught mid-breath. It was not all sharpness. There were traces of something else there, too; resilience, survival, even love, the complicated kind that grows in rooms where people have forgotten how to say it aloud. Still, whenever she entered that kitchen, her body remembered.

Shoulders tense. Breath measured. Hands steady. Because love, in that house, had always been something you learned to hold by the blade.

★ ☢ ★

It was Sunday night, and the table was set with her mother's usual precision. Every plate was centered perfectly on its place mat, each one aligned as if the table itself were a grid that tolerated no deviation. Forks and knives lay parallel, their handles measured to the same invisible line, so exact they might have been checked with a ruler. The napkins were folded once, with no extra creases, no softness allowed. One fold only. Clean. Final.

In the middle of the table sat a vase of tulips, trimmed short. "So they won't droop like apologies," her mother had said earlier, half-joking, half-warning, the scissors clicking shut with quiet authority. The petals were red and white, stark against the glass, like small flags of surrender pretending to be decoration. Eleanor noticed how the stems were cut unevenly beneath the waterline, hidden where no one would look.

Even order, she knew, had its concealed rough edges. Her mother believed in order. In symmetry. In the comfort of things that could be controlled. She believed in quiet meals and properly buttered bread, in chairs pushed in just so, in the choreography of small, correct gestures that kept chaos at bay.

She believed that if a table looked right, life might follow. But balance, Eleanor thought, was not the same as peace. Peace had warmth. Peace had room to breathe.

120

Balance, here, was just another kind of blade; sharp-edged, glittering, precise enough to draw blood without spilling a drop. The air carried the faint scent of roasted chicken, of starch and salt, of candles burned too long in a room that still felt cold. The refrigerator hummed steadily, filling the silences between sentences like a machine trained to cover discomfort.

Over it all, the kitchen clock ticked slow, insistent, a metronome counting down to the next polite exchange, the next safe topic. Eleanor sat straight-backed in her chair, hands folded neatly in her lap, her smile soft and practiced. She knew this posture. She had worn it for years. Across the table, her mother poured wine with the same care she applied to everything.

A steady wrist, a narrow stream, the bottle tipped at just the right angle at the end to catch the last drop before it could stain the cloth. "Drink?" She asked, already reaching for her own glass. "Not tonight," Eleanor said. Her mother nodded once, briskly, as if she had anticipated the answer and filed it away. The gesture was small, contained, and yet it rippled through the room like a stone dropped into still water.

Outside, the wind pushed against the windowpanes. The tulips trembled faintly in their vase. The candle flame wavered, then steadied again, a minor rebellion in a house that did not tolerate mess. Eleanor was seventeen. Nearly eighteen. Nearly free. The thought had become a quiet flame she carried in her chest, something warm and persistent that no amount of careful posture could extinguish.

She watched her mother cut into her chicken, the knife gliding smoothly, the fork steady, the motion rhythmic and soundless. It was almost beautiful, the way control could masquerade as grace. "You've been quiet lately," her mother said, her eyes still fixed on her plate. "Everything all right at school?" She asked. "Yes," Eleanor answered quickly. The lie slid easily across her tongue, smooth, habitual, barely felt. She had learned young that silence was safer than honesty, that peace in their house was a negotiation, not a gift.

Her mother nodded, chewing slowly, accepting the answer without truly hearing it. And Eleanor sat there, smiling softly, feeling the quiet flame inside her grow brighter, more certain, waiting for the moment when balance would no longer be enough. "Good," her mother said, setting her fork down with care, aligning it again with the edge of her plate. "You're close to graduating. These next few months are important."

"I know," Eleanor replied. The words were automatic, shaped by years of repetition. She kept her voice even, respectful, the way you speak when you don't want to invite follow-up questions. "Scholarships, deadlines, interviews," her mother continued, ticking them off as if reading from a checklist only she could see. "You can't afford distractions now. I just want you to be ready."

"I will be." She answered with ease. Her mother lifted her gaze then, just briefly, studying Eleanor the way she might study a résumé, searching for flaws, for gaps, for anything that might threaten the future she had already planned. A faint smile curved her mouth, careful and contained. "Good girl." The words were meant to be praise. They landed softly, almost kindly.

And yet their weight was sharp, pressing down in a way Eleanor felt immediately, like a blade laid flat against skin. Approval, she had learned, was never free. It always came with shape and expectation attached. Eleanor lowered her eyes to her plate. The chicken had cooled, the skin dulled, the steam long gone. She cut a small piece and chewed out of habit, though she could barely taste it.

The meal felt ceremonial now, something being performed rather than shared. The tulips leaned slightly toward the candlelight, their petals curling inward at the edges, their tips singed brown from standing too close for too long. Eleanor noticed how they strained toward warmth, even as it damaged them. She wondered if flowers knew when they were burning. Her mind drifted upstairs, to the notebook tucked beneath her pillow.

To the page she still didn't remember writing. *If you wish, the door is open.* She thought of how the words had felt when she first read them, like a hand reaching out in the dark, not pulling, not demanding, just waiting. An invitation, not an order. Everything her world was not. Her mother kept talking about calendars and logistics, about campus tours and housing forms, about futures arranged neatly like silverware in a drawer.

Eleanor nodded in the right places. She smiled when expected. She played her part well. But inside, the quiet flame grew stronger. It wasn't angry. It wasn't reckless. It didn't demand that she run or rebel or shout. It simply was steady, insistent, alive. It pressed against her chest like a second heartbeat, reminding her that something else existed beyond balance and approval. *Not yet,* it whispered. *But soon.* And for the first time, Eleanor did not shrink from its heat.

Because sometimes freedom begins not with running, but with sitting at a perfect table and daring silently to want more than balance. The thought settled into her like a decision she had already made and was only now admitting to herself. Eleanor felt it before she spoke, a tightening just below her ribs, a clarity that startled her with its calm. She lifted her eyes from her plate. The tulips, the candle, the aligned silverware, all of it blurred at the edges.

"Where's my father?" She asked. The words were quiet. Measured. But they landed with the force of something dropped from a height. They sat between them like a glass fallen onto the table; unbroken, but ringing, unmistakable. The sound of it seemed to echo off the walls, off the white paint, off every year of careful avoidance. Her mother's hand stilled on her fork. Not dramatically.

Not enough for anyone outside the room to notice. Just a pause, a hitch in the choreography of dinner, like a dancer missing half a beat. The knife hovered above the plate. The candle flame leaned, then righted itself. For a moment, Eleanor thought her mother might pretend not to have heard her. But then, calmly, almost conversationally, Lydia asked, "Why?" The word was precise. Clean. It did not rise or fall. It did not accuse.

It was the kind of question lawyers asked when they already believed they knew the answer. Eleanor swallowed. Her heart was loud in her ears, but her voice, when it came, was steady. "Because I want to know." She did not apologize. She did not soften it with "just curious or I was wondering." She let the sentence stand on its own. Her mother studied her then, really studied her, as if seeing the shape of her daughter anew.

Eleanor felt that gaze like a hand turning her face toward the light, searching for cracks. "You don't need to know," Lydia said finally, resuming her cut into the chicken. The knife slid cleanly. Too cleanly. "Some questions don't help." The blade pressed through the meat with quiet certainty. "That's not true," Eleanor said. The words surprised her with their firmness. She had expected her voice to waver, to give her away. It didn't. It held.

Her mother looked up again, eyes sharp now, reflective. "It is true," she replied. "Wanting something doesn't make it useful." Eleanor's fingers curled slightly in her lap. She thought of the flame in her chest. Of doors. Of keys. Of a name she had never been allowed to say. "I'm not asking for useful," Eleanor said. "I'm asking for honest." The refrigerator hummed louder, or maybe she was only noticing it now. The clock ticked. One second. Then another.

Lydia exhaled, slow and controlled the way she did when a conversation threatened to spill past its boundaries. "He left," she said. "That's all you need." She said with finality. "When?" Eleanor asked. Her mother's lips pressed together. "A long time ago." She responded with annoyance in her voice. "Why?" She continued her questioning. "Because he wasn't ready." Her mother said.

For what?" Eleanor leaned forward slightly, her hands finally coming to rest on the table. "For me?" She said with more questions than answers in her eyes. The question trembled only at the very end. She let it. Lydia's gaze hardened, not with anger, but with something colder. Final. "Eat your dinner," she said. "I'm not hungry." Eleanor said. "Don't do this." Her mother groaned. "I'm already doing it." She said with sharpness. The chair scraped softly as Eleanor shifted.

It sounded impossibly loud in the quiet kitchen. Her mother's jaw tightened, a familiar signal, the warning flare before control reasserted itself. "Your life," Lydia said carefully, "is the one I've given you." The sentence closed like a door. Eleanor felt it, not slam, but seal. "Sit down." Lydia warned. "No." Eleanor responded. The word was small. Absolute.

Behind her, the candle flickered. The tulips leaned further toward the heat. Eleanor recognized it the way some people recognize a childhood song, the rhythm ingrained, the meaning already known. Do not press. Do not dig. Let it pass. That silence had trained her. It had shaped her posture, her tone, the way she learned to swallow questions before they ever reached her tongue.

Most nights, it worked. But tonight, it didn't. The flame in her chest did not dim. It sharpened. "Is he alive?" Eleanor asked. The words were simple. Unadorned. There was no accusation in them, no plea. Just a need that had finally reached its breaking point. Her mother paused. Not long. Not dramatically. But long enough that Eleanor felt the air change, as if the room itself had inhaled and was waiting to see what would come next. Lydia chewed slowly, deliberately. Swallowed.

Then she set the fork down, aligning it perfectly with the knife, as though order could still be restored if she were careful enough. She dabbed her lips with the napkin. Once. Twice. Every movement precise. Controlled. Measured down to the smallest gesture. "Alive isn't the same as present," Lydia said. The words were delivered evenly, almost gently. They were meant to close the door without slamming it, to sound wise instead of evasive. Eleanor felt something cold slide through her chest.

"That's not an answer," she said. Her voice was steady. That surprised her. She had expected it to crack, to betray her. It didn't. Lydia looked up then, really looked at her. Her eyes were sharp, assessing, as if Eleanor had just crossed an invisible line and was now standing in unfamiliar territory. "It's the only answer you're going to get," her mother replied. Eleanor's fingers curled against the edge of the table. She could feel the grain of the wood beneath her skin, the shallow grooves worn by years of meals and elbows and unspoken things.

"You always do this," Eleanor said quietly. "You answer something else. Something adjacent. Something that sounds like truth but isn't." Lydia's mouth tightened. "I am protecting you." She said with no emotion. "From what?" Eleanor asked. "From him? Or from you?" Adding quietly. The candle flame wavered, leaning sharply to one side before steadying again. For a fraction of a second, so brief Eleanor might have imagined it, something raw flickered across her mother's face. Fear, perhaps. Or regret. Or the exhaustion of holding a story in place for too long.

Then it was gone. "You're tired, this is not the conversation to have on a Sunday night." Lydia said. "When would it be?" Eleanor pressed. "After graduation? After college? After I built an entire life without knowing where I came from?" Many more unanswered questions came up in her head. "That life will be better for it," her mother said, firmly now.

Eleanor shook her head. "You don't get to decide that." The silence that followed was different from the others. Not trained. Not rehearsed. It stretched, thin and unfamiliar, like fabric pulled past its limit. Lydia stared at her plate. Eleanor waited. For the truth. For a crack. For anything real. But none came.

And in that moment, Eleanor understood something with startling clarity: this silence was not protecting her. It was protecting the story. She pushed her chair back slowly, the sound of wood against tile loud in the stillness. "Then I'll find out myself," she said. Her mother did not look up. But the knives on the table caught the light all the same; sharp, gleaming, unmoved. Her mother's eyes lifted then, sharp as polished glass, finally fixing on Eleanor as if daring her to look away.

"The answer is that he left," she said. "That's what you need to know." The sentence landed with a practiced finality, the kind meant to end a conversation before it could become dangerous. Eleanor felt her pulse hammer in her throat, loud enough that she was certain it could be heard across the table. She swallowed once, steadying herself, and asked the question that had been pacing her ribs for years. "Did he take me?" The air between them cracked. Not loudly.

No shatter, no slam, but with the brittle snap of something held too long under pressure. The candle wavered. The refrigerator's hum deepened. Even the tulips seemed to stiffen, their petals catching the light like witnesses. For a single, unguarded heartbeat, her mother's face changed. Something raw flickered there; fear, maybe, or grief, or the memory of a choice that had never stopped costing her.

It was subtle, almost imperceptible, but Eleanor saw it. Saw the woman beneath the polish. Saw the wound. Then the mask slid back into place. Porcelain-smooth. Immaculate. Untouched. "Eat your dinner," Lydia said softly. The gentleness of it was worse than anger. Worse than shouting. It was control wrapped in calm, a command disguised as care. "I'm not hungry," Eleanor said.

Her voice surprised her, quiet, steady, unmoved by apology. Lydia's mouth tightened. "Don't play this game with me." Eleanor looked down at her untouched plate, the food cooling into irrelevance, and understood something with startling clarity: this was not a game. Games could be won or lost. Games ended. This was a line being drawn. And for the first time, Eleanor did not step back from it. "It's not a game." Eleanor pushed her chair in.

The scrape of wood against tile sounded too loud in the tight room, a sudden violence that made her flinch even as she caused it. Her hands shook, but she did not pull them into her lap. She let them hang at her sides, empty and honest. "It's my life." Her mother looked at her then, really looked, as if recalibrating, as if something in the script had gone off-book. Lydia's lips thinned, the line precise, deliberate. "Your life," she said, evenly, "is the one I've given you." The words fell with the weight of doors slamming down a long hallway.

Not one door. Many. Each shutting off a version of the world Eleanor had not been allowed to imagine. She did not answer. There was nothing left to say in that room that would not bleed. Eleanor turned and walked out of the kitchen, each step a quiet act of defiance. Upstairs, she closed her bedroom door with care, as if noise itself might betray her. She leaned her forehead against the wood and stayed there until her breathing slowed, until her heart stopped trying to escape her chest.

The navy notebook lay on her desk, exactly where she had left it. Waiting. She crossed the room and opened it with hands that trembled, the paper whispering softly as if it already knew. She flipped to a blank page and wrote quickly, before fear could interrupt. *I do not believe her.* The pen paused. Ink bled slightly at the end of the sentence.

Then, smaller, steadier: *I do not think so; the silence is over.* Below that, after a breath she didn't realize she'd been holding: *A lie told every day is still a lie.* The star-shaped necklace glinted in the lamplight, gold and sharp, a small borrowed constellation. Eleanor closed her fist around it until the metal pressed into her palm, until the pressure became grounding, undeniable. A mark bloomed there, faint but real. Her mother's version of the story had always been clean. Neat. Convenient. Miles left. Three words to explain away a lifetime.

But Eleanor's heart tuned like an instrument she had never asked to inherit, vibrated with a different truth. One that had been humming beneath everything, patient and persistent. That absence could be chosen, yes. But it could also be forced. That maybe, just maybe, somewhere a man was waiting. Writing. Hoping. Not gone, not careless, but kept away by forces larger than either of them had been at the time. That night, the flame pressed hard against her ribs, as though it knew time was running out for pretending.

The next morning, Lydia moved through the kitchen as if the night before had been nothing more than a wrinkle in fabric. Something easily smoothed. "I've scheduled your college tour," she said, pouring coffee. The mug did not clink against the counter. Nothing ever clinked. "Next Saturday. We'll make a day of it." Eleanor nodded. "Okay."

She said it because resistance before caffeine felt like wasted ammunition. Because she had learned the difference between choosing battles and surviving them. But inside, something set. If her mother built walls, Eleanor would look for cracks. If silence was the weapon, she would answer with questions. If truth had been buried, she would dig. That evening, she returned to the library.

She took her usual seat at the back of the computer lab, where the fluorescent light flickered faintly and no one bothered to glance over her shoulder. The hum of machines wrapped around her like a held breath. She typed **Miles Bennett** again, then paired it with her town's name, her mother's, her own. Names spilled across the screen. Most meaningless. Some unsettlingly close. She copied them into her notebook, each one a possible hinge, a potential key. Her hands trembled, not with fear alone, but with something dangerously close to hope.

If her mother's silence was the lock, this was her first turn of the key. The library was quieter than usual, the late hour thinning the crowd to a few scattered silhouettes bent over screens and books. Eleanor sat at her usual table, notebook open, pen idle in her hand, her attention drifting more than focusing. The air felt charged in a way she couldn't quite name, like something unresolved hovering just beyond her reach.

Someone slid into the chair across from her without asking. She looked up, startled, then relaxed when she recognized him, Evan, from choir, from shared rehearsals and borrowed pencils, from the small, unspoken familiarity of people who had been orbiting the same spaces for years without colliding. "You're always here," he said softly, almost amused, as if he'd just noticed a pattern he'd been tracking subconsciously. "So are you," Eleanor replied.

It came out steadier than she expected. He smiled, crooked and unsure, and for a moment neither of them spoke. The silence between them wasn't heavy. It was tentative. Curious. The kind that asks a question without forming the words. Evan leaned forward slightly, resting his elbows on the table. "You okay?" He asked.

Eleanor hesitated. The honest answer felt too large for the space between them. "Yeah, just thinking." She said instead. "You always are," he said, not unkindly. The words lingered. Something shifted, small, almost accidental. He reached out, fingers brushing hers where they rested on the edge of the notebook. The contact was brief, barely there, but it sent a clear, undeniable signal through her chest. She didn't pull away. Neither did he. It happened without ceremony. Without planning.

He leaned in, slow enough that she could have stopped it, and she realized, distantly, that she wasn't going to. Their lips met, soft, tentative, a question rather than an answer. It was quick. Awkward at the edges. His breath caught; so did hers. When they pulled back, neither of them spoke right away. Eleanor felt… something. But it wasn't fireworks. It wasn't clarity. It wasn't the door opening the way she had imagined doors opening. It was warmth, yes, but also distance. As if she had touched something adjacent to what she was looking for.

Evan smiled again, uncertain now. "I should…" he gestured vaguely toward the exit. "Yeah." Eleanor echoed, "Yeah." He left without another word. The chair across from her remained empty. Eleanor sat there for a long moment, fingers resting where his had been, trying to take inventory of what had changed. Her pulse was steady. Her thoughts were calm.

Whatever she had crossed just now, she knew instinctively, was not the threshold she had been circling. Still, she didn't regret it. She closed her notebook, stood, and walked out into the night carrying a new certainty: wanting contact was not the same as wanting connection. And not every door, she was learning, was meant to be opened just because it was closed.

At home, the tulips on the table had already wilted. Their petals drooped over the edge of the vase, red fading toward brown, the gold edges dull now, unremarkable. Eleanor paused before going upstairs and looked at them for a long moment. *Not even order lasts forever,* she thought. Later that night, Eleanor lay awake long after midnight, the world beyond her window washed in silver and sound. Rain had begun tenderly, testing the ground.

Now it fell with certainty, each drop against the gutter a heartbeat, a footstep, something approaching without yet knocking. She traced the ceiling cracks with her eyes in thin branching lines like rivers on an old map. In the glow of her nightstand lamp, the walls seemed to breathe, shadows swelling and receding in time with her pulse.

A half-burned candle flickered beside her, the flame leaning toward the open window, caught between staying and leaving. Her navy notebook lay open on the blanket, pages fluttering gently in the draft. The words stared back at her, darker now, as if rewritten while she wasn't looking. *If you wish, the door is open.* The graphite shimmered faintly, no longer just marks but something active, like a thought that had learned to stand on its own. She reached for the page, then stopped. The space between her fingers and the paper felt charged.

As though touching the sentence might complete a circuit she was not yet ready to close. The star necklace lay beside her pillow. She pressed it into her palm until the points marked her skin. When she opened her hand, the imprint remained, a small constellation, red and real. The house creaked in its sleep. Pipes sighed. The refrigerator hummed. Somewhere down the hall, her mother moved, distant as weather. Eleanor turned toward the window. Streetlights trembled in puddles.

Trees swayed like slow dancers. A passing car cast a brief wash of light across her wall, then moved on. She thought of him, not as a man yet, but as a possibility. *Miles Bennett.* A name that still felt half-borrowed. Half-found. She could not picture his face. It refused to stay still. But she could imagine his voice as quiet, careful. The kind that does not interrupt silence, but makes room inside it.

Tears arrived without warning, sliding into her hair, catching faintly in the light. She let them fall. This was not breaking. This was release. Her last thought before sleep was not careful or composed. It was small. Unguarded. Almost childlike. *Please let him be real.* The thought slipped outward, past her lips, past the glass, into the rain. She imagined it traveling along gutters and streets, carried by water until it reached another window.

In a small apartment across town, a man stirred from half-sleep, his hand brushing instinctively against the letter in his pocket. He did not know why he smiled. Only that something had called his name. The rain kept falling. The city held its breath. And somewhere between one heartbeat and the next, the distance between them finally began to give way.

That night, she dreamed of the door she had drawn a hundred times. Only this time, it opened a fraction wider. A hand reached through, unfamiliar, trembling, but steady, holding a single candle flame.

Eleanor woke with the word *Father* on her lips, the syllables warm and undeniable in the dark.

Eighteen Candles

Miles stayed where he was, hands resting flat on the table, palms open as if he might feel the future vibrate up through the wood. The flame bent and straightened again, obedient to currents he could not see. He thought of all the nights he had sat exactly like this, measuring time by wax and breath, by how long he could hold himself still without breaking. Back then, the candle had been a promise he made into emptiness. Now it felt like a signal, faint, uncertain, but sent.

He reached for the nearest box and lifted the lid, slow, reverent. The familiar scent rose immediately: old paper, graphite, a trace of smoke. He did not read any of the letters. He didn't need to. He knew them the way you know your own scars; by location, by pressure, by the memory of how they were made. He touched the top page with two fingers, just enough to remind himself that the years were real, that he had not imagined the discipline of staying. He closed the lid again and slid the box back into place, aligning it with the others.

Order mattered tonight. Not control, but order. A way of telling the universe he was ready to receive something without crushing it. The thought frightened him. Hope always did. Despair had rules. Hope had edges you could cut yourself on. He stood and crossed the room, pausing at the window. The glass was cool beneath his fingertips.

Below, the street lay rinsed and reflective, a second city trembling upside-down in the puddles. He imagined her somewhere in that reflected world, walking, breathing, carrying questions like loose change in her pockets. The idea that she might be awake at the same hour made his chest ache in a way that felt almost holy.

"Easy," he murmured to himself, the word barely sound. He had learned to speak gently when his heart began to run ahead of him. Eighteen years of waiting had taught him restraint the way monks learn silence, not as absence, but as practice. Behind him, the candle gave a soft, decisive flicker, as if answering something unspoken. Miles turned back toward the table. *Tomorrow,* he thought. *Or soon.* Soon was a word he had avoided for most of his life. Tonight, he allowed it to sit with him.

Outside, the wind moved again, stirring the halos in their puddles, rearranging the stars at street level. The city exhaled. Miles drew a breath that went all the way to the bottom of his lungs and stayed there a moment longer than usual. For the first time in years, he did not feel like a man keeping vigil alone. He felt like someone standing at the edge of an answer. Life was happening all around him, unknowing, unstoppable, and for the first time, he did not feel entirely outside of it.

The city had not paused for his sorrow or his discipline; it had kept moving, carrying strangers home, washing storefronts clean, breathing in and out without ever asking his permission. And somehow, tonight, that didn't wound him. It steadied him. It felt like an invitation rather than a dismissal. Miles opened the top box. The one marked **Year One.** The cardboard sighed softly, a tired sound, as if relieved to be opened again.

Inside, the letters lay stacked with careful reverence, their edges uneven from being folded and unfolded, held and released. The paper smelled faintly of dust and smoke and something sweet, not sugar exactly, but the ghost of hope, the residue of a promise made when he had almost nothing else to give. Miles lifted a letter. *My little star.*

The words looked smaller than they used to. Or maybe he had grown. Or maybe time had widened the space around them. He smiled faintly, a smile that tugged at one side of his mouth and nowhere else, the kind that comes when memory presses gently instead of hard. He had written those words enough times to teach them to stand, to breathe, to walk through years without him holding their hand. They had learned to carry weight. They had learned how to wait. They had learned how to survive silence.

But tonight was not about what he had written before. Tonight was not about preservation. It was about risk. Miles set the letter back into the box and closed the lid with care, as if tucking in something that had finally learned to sleep without fear. He drew a fresh page toward him with its blankness luminous under the candlelight, uncreased, unmarked, asking nothing of him except honesty. The page felt heavier than any letter he had ever written.

Blank pages always did. They contained possibility, and possibility was dangerous. His pen hovered, the ink trembling at the tip as if it, too, understood the risk of touching down. Beyond the window, the city flickered in fragments, in headlights sliding across brick facades, a bus sighing at the corner, the moon briefly caught between torn clouds before vanishing again.

Everything felt suspended, as though the night itself had leaned in to listen. Miles did not move. For so long, writing had been survival. Muscle memory. A ritual sharp enough to keep despair at bay. But this moment was different. This was not habit. This was not endurance. This was an answer forming. He felt it in his chest, that tight, electric ache that comes when truth finally decides it can no longer wait.

Somewhere out there, impossibly, unbearably, his words might land in hands that could hold them. Not as echoes. Not as prayers cast into dark. But as something received. A place to arrive. The candle wavered as a draft slipped in through the cracked window. The flame bent low, nearly horizontal, its light thinning to a trembling thread. For one breathless second, Miles thought it might go out, eighteen years reduced to smoke and absence.

"No," he murmured, not in anger, but in plea. He reached for the matchbook, hands steadying as if guided by instinct older than thought. He struck once, nothing. Struck again, the sulfur flared, sharp and sudden, blooming into heat. He cupped the flame with his palm and touched it to the wick. The candle caught. Gold flooded upward, small but resolute. The flame leaned in the draft, bowed once, then straightened like a quiet soldier standing guard against the dark.

Wax began its slow descent, pooling at the base like time melting into patience. Miles let out a breath he hadn't realized he was holding. He sat back down, the chair creaking softly beneath him, and leaned closer to the table. The fresh page waited, pale and vulnerable, the faint tooth of the paper visible in the candlelight. His pen rested there, uncapped, poised. For years, he had said the words only in whispers. To walls. To shadows.

To air that never answered back. Tonight, he let them have weight. *"Happy birthday, my little star,"* he whispered. His voice cracked, not loudly, not dramatically, but in the quiet, ordinary way of something worn thin by love. The sound seemed to surprise him. It echoed softly off the walls, settling into the room like a presence that had finally been invited inside.

He closed his eyes for a moment and pictured her
as she might be now. Taller. Sharper around the edges.
Carrying questions the way he carried faith, carefully, and
everywhere. He wondered if she knew how strong she
already was. If she had learned to make herself small to
survive, or if she had burned bright in spite of it. His hand
lowered. The pen touched the page.

Ink spread, decisive, irreversible. And as he began to
write, Miles understood something that made his chest
ache open, that this letter was no longer a vigil. It was a
threshold. A step forward instead of keeping still. Outside,
rain began again, light and patient, tapping at the window
like a reminder.

Inside, a man who had waited eighteen years finally let
himself hope that the dark might answer back.

Miles sat with the candle until the wax ran low, the
flame thinning to a trembling needle of gold. It wavered,
recovered, wavered again, the way a heart does when it
has carried hope too long to trust rest outright. Melted wax
pooled at the base in pale, uneven rings, and the air took
on the faint perfume of smoke and warmed paper, that
particular sweetness old letters carry when heat remembers
them. He did not move.

The silence around him hummed, not empty, never
empty. The radiator ticked in its sleep. The city breathed
through thin walls. Somewhere nearby, a television released
a soft burst of laughter that belonged to a life he did not
know, a life continuing without his permission. He did not
blow out the candle. He had learned that endings rushed
become wounds.

So he let the flame finish in its own time, surrendering
without force. The wick bowed, glowed once more, and
then quietly gave up its light. For a while, Miles sat in the
dark with his eyes closed, breathing the smoke. This was
not grief. Not longing. It was the hush that follows a long
vigil when the watcher senses without proof that dawn has
been scheduled.

When he opened his eyes, the room looked altered. The
shadows felt less sharp. The loneliness had softened, as if
it had finally been acknowledged and, having been seen, no
longer needed to shout. The letter lay on the table before
him. The ink was still damp. The words small. Certain. He
read them again by the diluted city glow seeping through
the blinds, his finger hovering just above the page, tracing
the sentence as if touch alone might wake it.

If you wish, the door is open. For eighteen years, he
had written around fear. He had explained. Apologized.
Offered context and weather and poetry, as if meaning
might accumulate through volume. Tonight, he had written
only truth. Sometimes love is not a flood. Sometimes it is
a single line of light beneath a door. He folded the paper
carefully, each crease slow and intentional, the sound soft
as a vow being laid down. Then, without reaching for the
shoe boxes, his reliquary of patience, he took out a clean
envelope. This one had no dust. No history.

Hope, he realized, has weight. Not heavy. Not light.
Living. He slipped the letter inside, sealed it with the flat of
his hand, and tucked it into the inner pocket of his jacket.
The fabric whispered, as though the paper had found breath
again. It felt different there. Not memory. Intent. He stood.
The chair legs murmured against the tile. The candle was
ash now. The shoe boxes watched from the table, lids half-
lifted like eyes that had already seen enough.

For the first time, he did not reach for them. He did not need to. The jacket rested heavy against his chest, as though the letter carried not just words, but the gravity of every year he had endured without her. He ran his fingers once along the pocket seam. This one was not meant to be stored. This one was meant to move. Outside, rain began again softly, uncertain drops tapping the glass in the same rhythm he had written to for nearly eighteen years.

A pulse shared by two lives waiting to meet in the middle. Miles turned off the light. The room disappeared, save for three streetlamps reflected in the window with three perfect circles of gold, hovering like witnesses. He did not pray. He did not need to. He whispered only one word into the dark, his voice steady, almost young again. *"Tomorrow."*

For once, it did not sound like hope. It sounded like arrival.

The First Word

Morning came not with trumpets, but with a quiet insistence. Light slid through the blinds in thin, forgiving stripes, dust motes drifting lazily in its path. The pipes groaned awake inside the walls, a low, reluctant sound like an old man clearing his throat. Somewhere above him, footsteps crossed the apartment ceiling slow, deliberate pacing, someone arranging the shape of their day before it had fully begun.

The kettle sputtered on the stove, its lid rattling like a coin shaken in a jar, impatient for heat. The air still carried the faint trace of last night's smoke, the ghost of a candle that had burned itself to silence. Wax had cooled into pale ridges along the tabletop, small hardened rivers marking where heat had once lived.

Outside, the rain had moved on, leaving the city rinsed and shining, streets slick as glass, as though the night had scrubbed itself clean of regret. Miles had not really slept. Sleep had come in fragments, five minutes here, a drifting there, the kind of half-rest that keeps a man tethered to his thoughts even while his eyes are closed. Each time he slipped under, he saw the envelope. Each time he surfaced again, it was still there, waiting on the chair beside his coat.

He sat now at the table, palms curved around a mug that was already cooling, watching steam curl and dissolve into the morning air. The coffee was bitter. He did not mind. It felt right, plain, honest. The envelope lay heavy in his jacket pocket, its edges softening where his thumb had pressed it through the fabric. He kept reaching for it without meaning to, as if the paper might disappear if left alone too long.

If you wish, the door is open.

He had never written anything so bare. So surrendered. Those words had cost him more than all the others combined. Now, in the gray hush of dawn, they no longer felt like a letter. They felt like an event. Like a hinge turning. Like something unseen had shifted its weight in the air. Miles rose and crossed to the window.

Below, the city was waking slowly, half-dreaming. Delivery trucks rolled through shallow puddles, their tires sighing. Pigeons gathered along telephone wires, clustered like thoughts that had not yet found sentences. On the corner, a shopkeeper unlocked his door and paused to stretch, breath blooming white in the cool air.

Miles touched the glass. His reflection layered itself over the world outside, his face older than he remembered, lined by years that had not asked permission, but softer too. The kind of face that had learned the difference between holding on and holding open. The letter in his pocket felt alive. Not warm exactly but pulsing with a quiet certainty. He could not explain it, only knew that it no longer belonged to him alone. It was a key now, waiting for the lock it matched. He thought of her. *Eleanor.* The name itself was a tremor in his chest, delicate and dangerous.

He imagined her somewhere under this same light, maybe still asleep, maybe standing at her own window unaware that the day had already begun to bend toward her. He turned from the glass and looked around the room. The table cluttered with old letters. The shoe boxes stacked like monuments to his patience. For years, this space had been both anchor and cell. This morning, it felt different. Not smaller. Thinner. As if the walls were no longer necessary to hold him. Miles picked up his jacket.

The paper rustled faintly as it shifted inside, that soft, electric sound like the breath before a confession. He slipped one arm into the sleeve, then paused, hand resting on the back of the chair, and took it back off. The world outside remained gray, but not the gray of sorrow. This was the gray of possibility. The color of a page waiting for ink. He breathed in slowly, tasting the last of the night on the air, and whispered, not a prayer this time, but a truth he had finally learned to trust. *"Some doors only open when you stop knocking."*

Later, he sat again at the table, palms curved around his mug as though warmth might teach him what to do with it. He had started drinking his coffee black years ago out of habit more than preference, a bitterness that matched his quiet mornings. But lately, he had given in to a small indulgence.

The bottle of Coffee Mate French Vanilla stood on the counter beside the sugar jar, its cheerful label slightly absurd against the plainness of everything else in his kitchen. He poured a little. Then, after a moment, a little more. White ribboned through the dark coffee, curling and dissolving like a cloud finding its place in the sky. Miles smiled a small, dry smile, self-aware. *"Guess I'm getting soft,"* he muttered to no one.

The sweetness surprised him, as it always did. Vanilla lingered faintly on his tongue, gentle and unexpected, a reminder that the world could still offer kindness without being asked. He leaned back, the chair creaking beneath him. His fingers drifted again to the jacket on the chair beside him, pressing against the pocket where the letter waited. He traced its outline through the fabric, grounding himself in its presence. It was still there. Still real.

He thought: *She's eighteen now.* The words landed with a weight that felt both heavy and holy. *Eighteen.* Old enough to choose. Old enough to ask. Old enough to forgive, or not to. He thought: *"If she ever wants me, she can come. If she doesn't, then at least she has the choice."* The thought did not break him. It steadied him. For the first time in years, he allowed the future to belong to her instead of to his regret.

Morning light shifted, catching the edge of the letter through the jacket fabric. The paper glowed faintly, as if it understood what it was about to become, not just a message, but an offering. Miles took another sip of coffee and grimaced, chuckling under his breath. "Too much vanilla," he said quietly, shaking his head. But he did not pour it out. He drank it anyway, sweet and imperfect and human.

He stood and slipped on the jacket. The paper crinkled against his chest, that electric sound again, like the world clearing its throat before speaking. And for the first time in years, the waiting did not feel like stillness. It felt like motion. A low hum beneath his ribs. A current gathering strength. It wanted to stand on a threshold. To turn a handle. To step through. The morning remained gray, but alive.

He turned the knob and stepped into the morning, where the soft, silver light that seemed to say: *"Go ahead."*

Across town, she woke to the sound of rain easing into sunlight, the kind of soft transition that makes the world look briefly forgiven. The drops had thinned to mist, the streets below her window glistening like fresh ink.

Steam curled up from the sidewalks, ghosting through the early light, the city exhaling after a long night of holding its breath. Eleanor lay still for a moment, listening. The radiators ticked. Somewhere above her, someone ran water and hummed faintly over the murmur of a morning show. Her own heartbeat kept time with the drip of gutters outside. Her birthday. *Eighteen.*

The word felt strange in her mouth. Too solid, too final, as if she had crossed into something irreversible while sleeping. As if the world had quietly shifted its expectations of her overnight. She sat up slowly, the blanket pooling in her lap, and took in her room. The walls were still layered with years of her sketches taped crookedly, postcards fading at the edges, corners curling where time had worried them thin. The navy notebook lay open on her nightstand, pages dense with doors.

The faint imprint of the star necklace still lingered in her palm, red dots fading like secrets into skin. The apartment smelled of coffee and lemon cleanser. Her mother was already gone. Or deliberately absent. On days that required tenderness, absence had always been her mother's chosen posture. On the kitchen table sat a single gift. A scholarship guidebook. Thick. Heavy. Wrapped in silver paper with mechanical precision, the kind of wrapping that looked less like celebration and more like containment.

A note was taped neatly on top in her mother's careful, disciplined handwriting: *Proud of you. Love, Mom.* The loops were restrained. The pressure even. Emotion ironed flat. Eleanor stood there longer than she meant to, looking at the book, the paper, the note, feeling the familiar pull between gratitude and grief. It wasn't a bad gift. It was exactly what her mother believed in: something useful.

Something forward-facing. A map for a life that began somewhere else. Still wrapped. Still controlled. Eleanor traced the word *Proud* with her finger, smudging the ink just slightly. "Me too," she whispered, not entirely sure what she meant. She turned toward the window. The light had changed into soft gold, threaded through the lingering mist. The air smelled of ozone and wet asphalt, that fragile scent the world carries when it is halfway between storm and calm.

She picked up the star-shaped necklace, cool against her palm. It had become a quiet talisman over the years, a compass she trusted more than certainty. She slipped it into her pocket and pressed her hand over it once for luck. Then she took the navy notebook, tucked it beneath her arm, and moved toward the front door. The scholarship guidebook stayed on the table. Wrapped. Perfect. Waiting. She paused at the threshold, listening to the city, the low roar of buses, a distant ferry horn, a dog barking two streets over.

Somewhere inside that noise was a rhythm she recognized but had never learned to name. Eleanor turned the handle. The door clicked softly behind her. The air met her face with warmth, the last mist catching in her hair. For the first time, she did not feel like she was leaving something behind. She felt like she was walking toward it.

The library welcomed her with cool air and the faint sweetness of paper and polish, that unmistakable perfume of dust, ink, and quiet ambition. Computer screens hummed in orderly rows, a soft mechanical chorus beneath the hush. Rain tapped gently against the tall windows, no longer urgent, just persistent. Drops gathered and slid down the glass in slow, shining paths, breaking the light into trembling silver lines.

Somewhere far away, thunder murmured like a memory clearing its throat. Eleanor took her usual seat at the back against the wall, half-shadowed, where no one looked twice. From here she could hear the librarian's shoes squeak, pages turning at long tables, the faithful heartbeat of the printer delivering someone else's certainty. She set her notebook beside the keyboard.

Brushed rain from her sleeve. Breathed. Her fingers settled on the keys. She typed slowly. **Miles Bennett.** The name looked too small to carry what it meant. Fragile and enormous at once, like the first step onto a bridge that might not hold. Her pulse climbed. For a moment, she almost deleted it. But the cursor blinked, steady, alive, waiting.

She added more. **Miles Bennett, Sierra Mesa, Arizona.** She pressed Enter. The screen hesitated. Loaded. Rearranged itself. Outside, the rain thickened. Somewhere, a child laughed, bright, defiant. Her grandmother's voice surfaced, tired and unguarded: *He stayed in Sierra Mesa after she left.* Another memory followed, sharper, her mother's anger cracking through the house: *He couldn't even keep a job at Desert Star Market.*

Eleanor's fingers moved. • **St. Augustine's Chapel** • **Desert Star Market.** Enter. The spinning wheel chased itself. The library hummed. Then… Results. Few. But enough. A faded community directory. Crooked banner. Old colors. She clicked. The page loaded slowly. Names. Numbers. And then, **Miles Bennett, Volunteer, St. Augustine's Chapel (Desert Star Market, Sierra Mesa Branch)** No photo. No story. Just a name. Eleanor's breath caught hard enough to hurt. Her vision blurred before she realized she was crying.

She tore a page from her notebook and wrote fast, too fast. The pen scratching, the letters uneven and desperate. Proof. Her hand shook as she flattened the paper. Three miles. That was all. Three miles of years and air and pavement. The distance between being lost and being found. She opened her email. The blank message window glowed white and merciless. Her reflection floated faintly in the glass, eyes wide, mouth trembling.

What could she say after eighteen years of silence? She typed then deleted. Typed again. Deleted. The cursor pulsed. Finally, she whispered, barely audible, *"Just start."* Her first attempt: *Are you my father?* Too sharp. Too exposed. Deleted. Second attempt: *I might be your daughter.* Too small. Too unsure. Deleted. Silence again. Her heart pounded so loudly she was certain it echoed.

Then she typed: *Hi.* Lowercase. Two letters. Nothing like the speeches she had written in her notebook over the years. Nothing dramatic. Nothing safe. Just an opening. She stared at it until it felt real. Until waiting felt heavier than sending. Her hand shook. She pressed Send. The sound was barely there, a soft digital sigh, but to Eleanor it was thunder. The word disappeared. Gone. Flying.

She sat frozen, breath shallow, heart slamming against her ribs. There was no undoing it now. The library continued around her with printers coughing, chairs shifting, a librarian clearing her throat, but Eleanor felt both weightless and anchored, suspended between one heartbeat and the next.

All of it narrowed to a single truth: *She had opened the door.*

★ ✿ ★

Hi.

He was sweeping the church hall when his phone buzzed. The broom moved in steady arcs, soft against the old pine floors. The scent of wax and candle smoke hung in the air, layered with faint traces of last night's potluck with coffee, chili, and something sweet that clung stubbornly to the walls no matter how often they were scrubbed. St. Augustine's was quiet that afternoon, emptied of voices, the kind of quiet that felt earned rather than abandoned.

Sunlight slipped through the stained-glass windows, breaking into fractured ribbons of blue and amber that crawled slowly across the pews as the day shifted. Miles leaned the broom against the wall and pulled his phone from his pocket, expecting another message from Miller's Market, a shift change, a reminder about stocking, a request to cover for someone who didn't want the late hours.

Instead, he saw a single notification. An email. No subject line. Just one word previewed beneath the sender's name. *Hi.* His thumb stilled above the screen. The church seemed to inhale around him. The radiator ticked once, then fell quiet. Somewhere deep in the building, a door settled on its hinge with a soft click. Even the light through the windows appeared to pause, suspended in color.

Miles stared at the screen longer than he meant to. The word was so small. So ordinary. The kind of word that passed between strangers every day without consequence. But this one… His chest tightened, sharp and sudden, as if something had reached inside and pressed a thumb directly against his heart. He swallowed. *"Get a grip,"* he murmured to himself, his voice sounding too loud in the empty hall.

Hi. He had written thousands of words to a girl who had
never answered. Years of pages folded into shoe boxes.
Carefully dated. Carefully restrained. And now, this. He
stepped closer to the nearest pew and sat, the wood creaking
softly beneath him. The broom slipped where he had leaned
it, clattering gently to the floor. The sound echoed down the
aisle like punctuation.

Miles held the phone in both hands now. He opened the
email. The screen bloomed white around the single word,
centered, unadorned. *Hi.* His breath came shallow. He read
it again. Then again, as if repetition might turn uncertainty
into certainty. For eighteen years, he had imagined what
this moment might look like. Long letters. Confrontation.
Anger. Questions sharp enough to draw blood. Not this.

Not two letters that felt like a knock on a door made
of glass. *"Okay,"* he whispered, not to the email, but to
himself. *"Okay."* His hands were shaking. He closed his
eyes, just for a second, and the image came unbidden: a
young woman sitting somewhere with the same light on her
face, her fingers hovering over a keyboard, her heart racing
the way his was now. *Eleanor.* The name moved through
him like warmth. He opened his eyes and glanced up at the
altar, the small wooden cross catching a sliver of sunlight.

He wasn't a man who prayed much anymore, not
formally, but habit and instinct bent him there all the same.
"Please," he said quietly, not sure to whom. *"Please let
me do this right."* His thumb hovered over the reply button.
He didn't type right away. Instead, he breathed. He thought
of the shoe boxes. Of the candle the night before. Of the
sentence folded into his jacket pocket like a vow. *If you
wish, the door is open.* The words felt different now, no
longer a hope sent into the dark, but an invitation someone
had actually answered.

He began to type, then stopped. Deleted. Tried again. He did not want to overwhelm her. Did not want to scare her back into silence. He remembered what it was like to be eighteen, to want answers but fear what they might cost. Outside, a bell rang once, just once, from somewhere down the street, marking the hour. Two letters sitting small and particular in the glow of the screen, unprotected by context or expectation. Miles stared at it, not breathing.

At first, his mind had reached for reason. A wrong number. A glitch. Spam slipping through a filter that had failed to do its job. The reflexes of a man trained by disappointment moved quickly, efficiently, trying to save him from hope before it could take root. But something in the way the word sat there stopped him. It wasn't the word itself. It was the weight inside it. The pause it carried. The courage required to send it without armor. His chest tightened, sharp and sudden. He read it once. Then again, slower this time, as if the meaning might change if he gave it room.

He read it until the letters lost their edges and became soundless shapes, until the hum of the lights overhead faded, until the creak of the rafters above the church hall disappeared entirely. All he could hear was that greeting echoing through the hollowed out years reverberating against eighteen birthdays, eighteen candles burned alone, eighteen years of writing into a silence that had never once answered back.

The broom slipped from his hand and clattered softly to the floor. The sound startled him enough that his knees nearly buckled. He stepped outside before he realized he'd moved, the door closing behind him with a gentle click that felt impossibly loud.

He sank onto the stone step, the cold seeping through his jeans, grounding him in a way nothing else could. The phone rested in his lap, glowing steadily, patient. The air smelled like rain soaked into dirt, the faint metallic tang left behind after a storm had decided it had done enough damage for one night. His eyes burned before he understood why. When the tears came, they did not rush. They arrived quietly, the way real things do, sliding down his cheeks without permission, without ceremony.

He pressed the heel of his hand to his mouth, a sound breaking free anyway, half laugh, half sob. For a long moment, he did not move. He sat there with his palms open, the phone resting between them like something sacred, something that had finally chosen him back. Eighteen years of silence, broken by two letters and a trembling courage. He could see her, not the infant he had memorized into ache, but someone grown now.

Someone standing somewhere in the world with shaking hands and a racing heart, brave enough to press Send without knowing what would come next. *"You did it,"* he whispered, voice cracking as if the words themselves were fragile. *"You really did it."* The phone waited. The cursor blinked. A heartbeat. He typed. Deleted and typed again. Each version felt too large, too heavy with the years she had not lived beside him.

His thumbs trembled. His breath kept breaking, catching in his chest like it had forgotten how to move forward. At last, he stopped trying to explain himself. Stopped trying to compress eighteen years into something survivable. He typed the only reply that felt honest enough to stand on its own. *Hi.* Nothing more. He stared at it for a long time, afraid that adding anything would tip the moment into something it wasn't ready to be.

Afraid that silence, once broken, might punish him for impatience. Then he pressed Send. The message disappeared with a soft whoosh, so quiet it could have been mistaken for nothing. But to him, it was the sound of the world splitting open and beginning again. Miles leaned back against the stone wall of the church, the late light spilling across his shoes, warm and ordinary and miraculous all at once.

Somewhere nearby, bells began to ring, not for a service, not for a ceremony, but as if the city itself had chosen that moment to mark what had just happened. Miles closed his eyes, the phone still warm in his hands. *"Thank you,"* he whispered to the silence, to the waiting, to the girl brave enough to say hello. Somewhere across the city, a girl would soon see his reply.

The wind carried the word away, soft and certain, toward whatever came next.

Eleanor was still in the library when the response came. She was not even looking at her phone. It lay face down beside her notebook, inert and ordinary, silent for so long that she had already begun rehearsing disappointment, telling herself this was what courage sometimes earned: nothing.

She had slipped her notebook into her bag and pushed her chair back, the soft scrape against the floor sounding too loud in the hush. A few students glanced up, then returned to their screens. The world remained intact. Then... *The vibration.* A low hum against the wood of the table. Once. Then again.

Her pulse leapt so violently it startled her. Eleanor froze, hand still wrapped around the strap of her bag, her body caught mid-decision. She stared at the phone as if it were something alive, something that might flee if she startled it. Her reflection hovered faintly on the dark glass, wide eyes, parted lips, a face suspended between disbelief and prayer. Don't rush it, she thought. Don't scare it away. Her fingers finally closed around the phone. It was warm. She turned it over. A new message. *Hi.* Two letters. The same two she had sent.

No punctuation. No explanation. Just that, clean and unmistakable. A mirror held up across eighteen years. For a moment, Eleanor forgot how to breathe. The library seemed to recede, the long tables and shelves dissolving into color and soundless motion, like a painting left out in the rain. All that remained was the glow of the screen and the sudden, impossible awareness that someone, *he,* was on the other side of it.

Her throat tightened painfully. Her hands shook so hard the phone nearly slipped free. She caught it against the edge of her notebook, heart hammering against her ribs, loud enough she was sure someone must hear it. The screen's light spilled across her fingers, illuminating a faint smudge of ink still clinging to her thumb, evidence of how recently her life had been divided into before and after. She reread the message. Again and again. Each time it shifted shape.

A greeting. A confirmation. A bridge was laid plank by careful plank. Her breath broke loose in a sound that startled her; half laugh, half sob, small enough to be swallowed by the room. She clamped her lips together, eyes burning, and pressed her free hand to her chest as if to steady her heart. She closed her notebook slowly and held it against herself, the familiar weight anchoring her.

The edges dug gently into her palms, grounding her in the present, in the fact of her own body. *"It's real,"* she whispered, barely moving her mouth. *"He's real."* No one looked up. The librarian continued shelving returns, methodical and unbothered. Somewhere, a printer whirred. A student turned a page. The ordinary world carried on, blissfully unaware that something irreversible had just happened in the far back corner.

Outside the tall windows, the Arizona light was changing. The clouds thinned and parted, and the sun struck the mesa beyond town, igniting it into copper and gold. The wet pavement caught the brightness and threw it back in fractured reflections, as if the city itself were trying to remember how to shine. Eleanor stood, notebook tucked under her arm, phone warm in her hand. Her knees felt weak, unreliable, like they might fold under the weight of what she now carried.

For eighteen years, silence had been her inheritance. It had shaped her, trained her, taught her how to listen. Now it had answered back. And she did not know yet what she would say next, but for the first time in her life, she knew she would not be speaking into the dark. Two *Hi's*. That was all. But between them stretched eighteen years of longing, silence, and a love that had never stopped breathing, only learned how to wait.

It had learned patience the way the desert learns endurance: slowly, painfully, without spectacle. Two letters from her. Two from him. Four minor characters were asked to shoulder the weight of almost eighteen years. It did not seem possible that so little could carry so much, and yet it did; perfectly, impossibly, like a bridge spun from thread that somehow held.

On one screen, a trembling girl in a desert town, her fingers still faintly scented with graphite and ink, her pulse loud in her ears, her chest tight with the unfamiliar sensation of being answered. On the other, a man seated on the worn stone steps of St. Augustine's Chapel, sunlight spilling across his knees, the phone resting in his hands as though it were something alive. His chest felt hollowed out and filled all at once, disbelief and joy sharing the same fragile space.

Two worlds. Two hearts that had lived entire lives apart, parallel, unseen, unknowable. Now, suddenly, miraculously, they were connected by the soft hum of a signal invisible as prayer. No witnesses. No ceremony. Just air and light and the quiet insistence of a connection refusing to be denied. If someone had been watching from far above, they might have seen it then: two tiny points of light flaring in the same instant, traveling through miles of heat and pavement and memory to meet somewhere unseen.

A convergence without spectacle. A miracle that did not announce itself. Two candles lit at opposite ends of the same table. Two stars are finally recognizing the shape of the sky. The message itself was small: *Hi.* But its echo stretched wide as the desert. Wide enough to hold every birthday missed, every letter written and never sent, every whispered prayer released into rooms that did not answer.

Eleanor pressed the phone to her chest, eyes closing, as if holding it there might steady her heart, or keep it from flying apart. Miles, miles away, did the same. Neither spoke. Neither moved. And yet, in that shared silence, something irrevocable shifted. A hinge turned.

A breath was taken.

A door long closed began, at last, to open.

The Meeting

They chose the café because it was ordinary. Neutral ground. Safe. A place with chipped mugs, wobbly tables, and a mural of sunflowers fading on one wall. The kind of place where no one expected miracles, only caffeine, small talk, and a little warmth to carry into the afternoon. Outside, Sierra Mesa carried on at an unhurried pace. The air shimmered with leftover heat from the night before, and a dry breeze stirred the smell of creosote and pastry through the open door each time someone entered.

The bells above the frame gave a tired little jingle that sounded more like memory than welcome. He arrived early. Too early. Miles had meant to wait until ten minutes before the hour, but his nerves betrayed him. He was there thirty minutes ahead of time, sitting at a corner table where he could see the entrance without looking like he was watching it. The server had offered him a smile that did not reach her eyes, the smile reserved for regulars and the lonely.

He ordered a black coffee, then changed his mind at the last second. "French Vanilla," he said, his voice catching, almost embarrassed. "The liquid kind. The one in the red bottle, if you have it." She nodded. "Coffee Mate?" Miles smiled. "Yeah. That's the one." Now the cup sat in front of him, untouched. The steam had thinned to nothing. The coffee had gone cold before he realized he had not even taken a sip.

His hands stayed wrapped around it, anyway, holding to its shape as though it were a lifeline. The café was filled with the small music of living, spoons stirring, the low hiss of the espresso machine, the faint hum of conversation. Somewhere near the counter, someone laughed, the sound like a glass wind-chime.

Every time the door opened, his body jolted, a reflex older than thought. His heart leapt like it had trained for this moment all its life, ready to sprint, ready to break, ready to believe. He thought of running. He thought of staying. He thought: *Please, let her come.* The clock on the wall ticked too loudly, its secondhand jerking forward with the authority of time itself. Miles had spent eighteen years writing words that might never be read, and now every second felt like a question: Will she? Won't she?

Through the café window, he could see the world carrying on, a delivery truck rumbling past, a man walking a dog, two teenagers sharing a milkshake at the curb. Life did not pause for miracles. Miles rubbed his thumb along the lip of his mug, the movement steady, nervous. His reflection trembled faintly in the dark liquid, and for a moment, he barely recognized the face staring back, older, lined, softer around the edges. The bell over the door jingled again. Miles looked up. And this time, he did not have to wonder.

Eleanor stood outside the café for ten minutes, the star necklace warm in her pocket from how tightly she had been holding it. The metal had left a faint imprint against her palm, a constellation of tiny points, red and trembling, as if courage could bruise. The air in Sierra Mesa shimmered with late-morning heat, the kind that made even shadows look uncertain.

Across the street, a pickup rumbled by, its radio spilling a country song into the stillness. Somewhere down the block, a wind chime stirred lazily in the breeze, its hollow notes falling like questions she could not yet answer. The café's sign, Mesa Bean & Bakery, squeaked on its chain each time the door opened. The bell above it gave a tiring little jingle.

She watched people come and go: a pair of elderly women in wide-brimmed hats, a young father balancing a coffee cup and a toddler on his hip, a teenager in an apron carrying a tray of croissants to the window display. All of them were so ordinary, so unaware of how extraordinary this morning felt to her. Eleanor wondered how many of them carried secrets as heavy as hers. How many hearts walking through this desert town beat around absences shaped like names.

The glass door reflected her face back at her, the kind of reflection that never told the whole truth. Her eyes looked too wide, her mouth too still. She looked older than she felt, younger than she wanted to be. The desert light had a way of stripping everything bare, even the things you wished would stay hidden. Her stomach fluttered, light and queasy. She pressed her hand to it, half expecting to steady herself, half hoping to quiet the noise inside. *He is just a man,* she told herself. Not a ghost. Not a story. *Just a man.*

But her legs did not believe her. They trembled anyway. The phrase *just a man* echoed in her mind, thin as paper. Because she knew the truth: *he had never been just anything.* He was the silhouette behind every question her mother refused to answer. The missing figure in her childhood drawings. The ache at the edge of every song she had ever sung about belonging. She closed her eyes.

The metal of the door handle was warm under her fingers, the heat of it seeping into her skin. The hum of the espresso machine carried through the glass, a low, steady rhythm like a heartbeat on the other side of fear. The bell over the door jingled as someone left, and for an instant, she almost slipped through in their wake, back into the safety of indecision, back into the comfort of not knowing.

But the moment passed, and something steadier rose in
her, not confidence exactly, but the ache of needing to find
out. Eleanor took one slow, deliberate breath. Then she
pushed the door open. The air inside was more incredible,
rich with the scent of cinnamon and roasted beans. Light
caught on the chrome espresso machine, on the curve of
mugs stacked along the counter, on the faint steam rising
from a milk pitcher.

She crossed the threshold, her hand still in her pocket
around the star necklace, a small, burning sun she carried
with her into whatever moment was going to be. When
she looked up, she saw him. Miles knew her the second
she stepped in. Not from her clothes, a simple blue dress,
scuffed shoes, or from her hair, which caught the morning
light like something half-remembered. No, it was the way
she paused in the doorway, scanning the room as if she
were looking for a ghost but expecting not to find one.

That careful searching, practiced by hope, looked like
caution. He knew it. It was his own. For eighteen years,
he had imagined this moment a thousand ways. He had
thought he might not recognize her. But the instant he saw
her, the world drew breath and stilled. He knew. She moved
one step forward, hesitant, her hand still buried in her
pocket where the star necklace waited.

The bell above the café door gave a small sigh as it
settled back into place, and the sound marked the boundary
between before and after. Miles rose without realizing
it. The chair legs scraped softly against the tile, a slight,
human sound that somehow carried the weight of years. His
heart was pounding so hard he could feel it at his fingertips.
And then, their eyes met. It was not exactly cinematic.
There was no swell of music, no rush of dialogue.

Just quiet recognition, the shock of something long lost returning most ordinarily. Her eyes were the color of the Arizona horizon before rain, that dusky blue that holds both hope and weather. They widened as she saw him, and within a heartbeat, she looked ready to turn and run. Eleanor stopped halfway to the table. Frozen. The café around them went on as if nothing sacred were happening, the hiss of the espresso machine, the soft murmur of conversation, a spoon clinking gently in a cup.

The smell of cinnamon sugar hung in the air, warm and faint. A ceiling fan turned lazily above, pushing the heat into slow circles. For a breath, for an entire world, neither of them moved. Miles' hands twitched at his sides. He wanted to speak, to rush forward, to tell her everything he had held inside every letter, every silence, every missed birthday. But when he finally found his voice, it came out small, reverent, a prayer. *"It's you,"* he whispered.

The words fell between them like light breaking through water. Eleanor's throat tightened. Her shoulders lifted with a shuddering inhale. For a moment, she looked as though speech might undo her. Her eyes glistened, not with tears yet, but with the weight of too many unsaid things gathering all at once. She nodded, once, barely, a movement so fragile it could have shattered if touched.

Her lips parted, trembling slightly, and then she said the only word that could carry them both across the impossible distance of years. "Hi." The same word that had started it all. And somehow, in that single syllable, in the way it quivered and steadied, in the way it filled the space between them, was everything: *the loss, the longing, the forgiveness neither had dared to believe was possible.* They sat.

Silence stretched at first, awkward and holy all at once. He wanted to spill everything, eighteen years of letters, candles, prayers. But his voice failed him. Eleanor wanted to demand answers, to know why absence had been her inheritance, but the words stuck like stones in her mouth. So, they began with fragments. "I thought about you every day," he said at last. His hands shook as he placed a folded piece of paper on the table, the newest letter, not yet stored in a shoe box. "I don't expect this to mean anything yet. But it's yours."

She touched the envelope with just her fingertips, as if it might burn. "You wrote to me?" She said with surprise in her voice. "Hundreds," he said, voice breaking. "Boxes full. Birthdays. Christmases. Every day I could. I… I couldn't be there, but I tried to make sure you'd never think I forgot." Her breath shuddered. "Mom said you left." His jaw tightened, but he did not reach for excuses. "I didn't leave you. I lost the fight. I was poor. I was broken. I was not what the law called stable. But I never left. I never stopped being your father."

Silence again. Eleanor studied his face, the lines at his eyes, the stubble at his chin, the way his mouth trembled when he tried to hold steady. Something in her chest, long walled, cracked. "I don't know what to do with this," Eleanor admitted. Her voice was soft, a confession.

"You don't have to do anything, we can go as slow as you need. Letters. Coffee. Nothing, if that is what you decide. I just want you to know the door is open. Always." He said quickly. The server came by and poured water into glasses. Neither of them touched theirs. The sound of the café swelled around them, murmured conversations, silverware clinking, the grind of beans.

Life was going on as if nothing world-shattering was happening in the corner booth. But for them, the air was charged, like lightning had decided to live in their lungs. Finally, she whispered, *"I think I've been waiting to hear that."* He exhaled as if he had been holding his breath for eighteen years. His eyes brimmed, but he did not look away. "Then maybe we're both here at the right time."

When they parted that afternoon, neither spoke of forever. Neither tried to name what this was. Words like always and never felt too fragile, too presumptuous for people still learning how to exist in the exact moment again. The air between them held a different kind of promise, quieter, human, trembling at the edges. The kind that does not need to be spoken to be true. He reached into his jacket pocket and pulled out an envelope. The paper had softened at the corners, the ink faintly smudged from the heat of his hands.

He hesitated for a moment, not because he doubted her, but because after all these years of writing to a ghost, he was suddenly standing in front of the person who made those letters real. His hand trembled slightly as he held it out. "It's… one of them," he said, his voice low. "The first, I think. I thought you should have it." Eleanor took it with both hands, as if accepting something sacred. The paper was warm, faintly scented with the coffee and candle wax that followed him.

She could see where it had been folded and refolded, where a corner had worn thin. She tucked it against her chest, just above her heart, as though it might steady the wild rhythm beneath her ribs. Her fingers brushed the edge of the envelope once, gently, afraid to crease it further. Neither of them said goodbye. Goodbye felt too much like the past, too final, too old a habit.

Outside, the rain that had lingered all morning had finally moved on. The sun broke through the clouds, a sudden, impossible gold spilling over the wet pavement. The street gleamed like glass, and puddles caught the light like small, liquid mirrors. The café windows reflected the sky, half storm, half promise. Eleanor stepped out into the warmth, blinking against the brightness. The air smelled of wet dust and cinnamon from the bakery next door.

Cars passed slowly through the shimmering heat, their tires whispering through shallow puddles. She turned once at the corner. Through the window, she could still see him, Miles, sitting at the same corner table, his coffee untouched, the chair across from him still slightly angled toward where she had been. His head was bowed. His shoulders shook, not violently, but in that quiet way that means a body has remembered how to cry.

His hands were pressed to his face as if in prayer, or gratitude, or both. The light caught the back of his hair, turning it silver at the edges. Something in her chest shifted, a slight, careful rearranging of ache and understanding. For the first time in her life, she thought: *I may not be alone in missing what I never had.* The thought was not sad. Not exactly. It was soft, fragile, almost tender like the beginning of something new.

She looked down at the envelope again, tracing the faint crease along its edge. The paper seemed to pulse faintly with warmth, as if it remembered the hand that had written it, the years it had waited to be read. Eleanor slipped it carefully into her bag, adjusted the strap on her shoulder, and began to walk. The light fell around her like a blessing, bright, forgiving, endless.

Behind her, inside the café, the man who had once been a story was still sitting in the glow, whispering something she would never hear. But she did not need to.

Because somehow, even though the distance, she felt it as a single truth, steady as heartbeat, a message carried in the air between them:

You were never forgotten.

The World Between Them

They met again three days later, in the park where the benches curved around a fountain and the trees leaned in like patient listeners. The place felt made for second chances, an in-between space where the city's noise softened into the language of water and wind. The sun had dropped low, turning the air honey-thick with late summer. The light pooled gold on the fountain's rim, glinting off coins that shimmered like trapped wishes.

Children's laughter drifted from the playground across the path, bright and careless, and the scent of cut grass lingered in the air, sweet and faintly wet. Eleanor arrived first this time. She sat at the edge of the fountain, hands folded in her lap, the star necklace resting between her palms like an anchor. She had worn a white dress that fluttered around her knees when the breeze passed, too formal for a park, too hopeful to admit.

Her heart was steady only because she had rehearsed calm in the mirror that morning, whispering, *"He's your father. He is just a person. He is your father."* Miles appeared from the far side of the path, a paper bag in one hand, the other shoved deep into his pocket. He had traded his work shirt for a clean one, though the sleeves were still rolled up, showing the dark tan of his forearms and the minor nicks that only labor gives.

There was nervousness in his gait, a stiffness in the shoulders, as if he were still learning how to inhabit this new kind of daylight. When he saw her, he stopped just short of the bench and exhaled through a shaky smile. "You beat me," he said softly, voice cracked at the edges. "I wanted to make sure it wasn't a dream," she replied, standing to meet him.

He held up the paper bag, sheepishly. "I brought something." Inside were two lemon muffins, slightly squashed, imperfect, still warm. "From the bakery near the church," he said. "They reminded me of something I once promised I'd learn to make." Her breath caught. "Lemon's my favorite," she said, the words quiet, reverent. "I know," he answered. Then, after a pause, "I always hoped it would be." They sat on the bench together, the fountain murmuring behind them.

The air between them hummed, not awkwardly, but like a wire strung between two points, carrying something invisible but strong. For a while, they did not talk. They just listened to the rustle of leaves, the far-off bark of a dog, the lazy hum of cicadas tuning the evening. Eleanor peeled back the muffin paper, broke a piece, and handed it to him. "We can share," she said, smiling faintly. Their fingers brushed. The contact was light, almost nothing, and yet both froze.

Miles looked at her then, really looked. The slope of her cheek. The faint freckle near her temple. The way the evening sun touched her hair. "You have your mother's mouth," he said quietly, "But your eyes… they're mine." She nodded. She did not flinch. The fountain burbled on, catching the last of the light, and for a moment the whole park seemed to breathe with them, two lives long divided, finally finding the rhythm of belonging again.

Eleanor rested one hand on the envelope folded in her lap, its creases softened by how many times she had opened and closed it. She lifted her eyes. "Why didn't you fight harder?" The question landed softly, but it did not miss. Miles flinched as if struck. He inhaled once, sharp and controlled. "I did fight," he said, then shook his head. "No. That's not enough."

He told her about the court. About being twenty-two. Broke. Afraid. Counting change for gas. About how love was never the question, stability was. About the gavel and the door it seemed to seal shut between them. "I told myself I was protecting you," he said. "That I needed to build something solid first. But all I gave you was absence." Silence followed, heavy and unjudging. "So you chose waiting," she said quietly. "Instead of coming." He bowed his head. "Yes."

The word barely survived his throat. "And it was the worst mistake of my life." The fountain hissed. Somewhere, a child's bicycle bell rang."I don't know how to forgive you," Eleanor said at last. Her voice trembled, but it held. "But I think… I want to try." Miles closed his eyes. Air left him in a sound that was half prayer. "That's more than I deserve," he said. "But it's everything I've ever hoped for." Neither reached for the other.

They stayed where they were, letting the moment exist without demanding more from it. The light shifted. The sky slid toward violet. Streetlamps flickered on, soft halos rising from the dark. "I need time," Eleanor said, standing. Miles rose slowly. "Take all of it," he said. "Just… don't shut the door." She nodded once.

Then she turned and walked away, the gravel crunching beneath her shoes, the envelope pressed to her chest. At the edge of the path, she stopped and looked back. He was still there. Sitting on the bench. Waiting. For the first time in her life, she did not look away. And beneath the deepening sky, the hinges loosened.

★ ◉ ★

Miles remained on the bench long after Eleanor disappeared down the path. The park emptied around him in stages. Families drifted away. Laughter thinned. The fountain's voice grew louder in the quiet, steady and indifferent, water rising and falling without concern for what had just been said beside it. He did not follow her. That restraint felt new. Earned.

For eighteen years, his instinct had always been pursuit disguised as patience, waiting that hoped to be rewarded for its endurance. Tonight, he understood the difference. Waiting was no longer something he did *to* time. It was something he gave *to* her. He looked down at his hands. They were trembling now that there was nothing left to hold together. The truth had cost him more than he expected. Not the telling of it, he had rehearsed that pain endlessly, but the way she had received it.

Without shouting. Without absolution. Without turning away. She had let the truth exist between them without trying to soften it, and that, more than anger, left him undone. "I don't know how to forgive you," she had said. He did not need forgiveness to breathe. But knowing she might someday *try* cracked something open in him he had sealed for survival.

Miles leaned forward, elbows on his knees, hands clasped loosely now instead of locked. His shoulders shook once, quietly, and then again. He pressed his mouth closed, not to stop the sound, but to keep it from becoming something performative. This grief was his. It did not need witnesses. The fountain caught the lamplight, scattering it across the stone in brief, trembling halos.

Coins winked beneath the surface, wishes dropped by strangers who would never return to see if hope remembered them. He thought of the shoe boxes waiting at home. The years cataloged and stacked. For the first time, they did not feel like proof. They felt like history, finished, complete, no longer the only evidence he had ever existed as a father. Miles straightened slowly. The bench creaked beneath him.

His knees protested when he stood, a reminder that time had not been suspended just because something sacred had happened. He did not look for her again. He trusted the space he had left her. As he walked away from the fountain, the air cooling against his skin, he carried something lighter than hope but stronger than regret. A quiet, unremarkable certainty: *She had not closed the door.*

And this time, he would not mistake stillness for love.

Relearning Love

A few days passed before Miles brought her anything else. They did not speak much during that time. No long explanations. No assurances. Just short messages. Neutral hours. The quiet agreement that what had opened between them in the park needed air before it could be handled. Eleanor did not ask for proof. Miles did not offer it. And yet, when he appeared at the café the following week with a large paper bag folded flat at the top, held carefully in both hands, she understood that this was not an argument. It was an offering.

The morning light came through the window in long gold stripes, falling across the space between them. He did not push. He did not ask her to open it there. He just placed the bag on the table with both hands, careful, almost reverent, as though it might break under the weight of what it carried. "Whenever you're ready," he said softly. His voice trembled in the quiet way that made her want to look away, not from discomfort, but because something in her already knew what it meant to hold back tears.

His hands shook as he slid the bag toward her, fingers brushing the edge of the table. It was not just an object he was passing through the distance. It was a lifetime, a heartbeat, the record of a love that had survived in exile. Eleanor stared at the bag, the brown paper creased and soft from handling. For a moment, she could not move.

Her pulse thudded in her ears, too loud. She nodded, said thank you because it was the only safe word she could find, and carried the bag out into the sunlight, as if it might vanish if she looked away. At home, she placed it on her bed and sat beside it for hours.

The afternoon light shifted across her room, from white to gold to the thin gray of evening, but still, she did not touch it. She simply watched it, her reflection flickering faintly in the brass knob of her dresser, the image of a young woman caught between wanting to know and fearing what knowing would undo. The paper bag looked harmless. Ordinary. The kind you could tear and throw away. But it hummed in the air like something was alive, something waiting.

Finally, as night began to press at the windows, she reached out. Her fingers brushed the edge of the paper, hesitated, then pulled it open. Inside was a single shoe box, old, softened at the corners, its cardboard dulled to the color of worn linen. The lid had been taped once, long ago, where a corner had split; the tape was yellow and barely holding. Across the top, written in faded ink in a hand she now recognized as his, was a single phrase: *Year One.*

The lid stuck for a second, as if it didn't believe it was allowed to be opened. When it finally lifted, a thin strand of tape peeled with it, releasing a smell that didn't belong to her room: candle wax, cheap coffee, and something like cold rain trapped in cardboard. Eleanor's breath hitched. She sat cross-legged on her bed, hands trembling as she lifted the lid. The faint scent of dust and paper rose up beneath it, as if the box had been sleeping for years and had only just remembered how to breathe.

Inside were folded pages, dozens of them, stacked carefully in layers like pressed flowers. Some edges were curled, some stained faintly at the corners where fingertips had lingered. Each one was dated. Each one began with the exact three words: *My little star.* She ran her thumb along the top sheet.

The paper felt thin, fragile with age, but the ink still held, dark and sure, like a pulse that refused to fade. Her chest tightened. She could feel the humming beneath her fingertips, every sleepless night, every hope written down and folded shut. Eleanor unfolded the page slowly. The paper resisted at first, stiff from years of being folded into itself, then gave way with a faint sound like breath.

The handwriting was smaller than she expected, uncertain, the lines pressing too hard in places as if the pen had hesitated mid-thought. She did not read past the first sentence. Her throat tightened, and she held the page still, letting her body register what her mind was not ready to absorb yet.

The letter began simply:

✱ ⚷ ✱

My little star,
Tonight, the world feels too quiet. If I write enough words, I might build a bridge strong enough for you to cross back to me. I do not know how to be a father from a distance, but I will try anyway. These words can hold what my arms cannot.

✱ ⚷ ✱

Her throat closed. She pressed her palm over the page, as if she could touch the version of him who had written it. The paper warmed beneath her hand. She could feel him there, eighteen years ago, tired, scared, still choosing to love. She read without counting.

Pages moved from top to bottom, then into her lap, then to the floor. Dates blurred. Her eyes burned. Her fingers cramped from holding the paper too tightly. Somewhere between one letter and the next, time stopped behaving like time and began behaving like weight.

By the time she reached the middle of the stack, the lamp on her nightstand had gone dim, and the room was all shadow and paper and breath. The handwriting was steadier there, the words slower, almost prayerful:

*   ✱ ⛤ ✱

I missed your first steps today. You haven't taken them yet. You are still learning how to stand. I am, too. But I promise you, someday when you walk toward me, I will still be here, learning how to meet you halfway.

*   ✱ ⛤ ✱

The sob broke before she could stop it. Eleanor pressed the letter to her chest. The words blurred into fabric, into heartbeat, into something larger than time. She whispered into the dark, her voice shaking but sure, *"I'm walking, Dad. I'm walking now."* And in the hush of the room, she could almost feel him answer.

She unfolded another letter, the paper trembling between her fingers. The ink had bled a little in places, as if the rain had once found it, or tears. The handwriting was uneven, shakier, younger, less sure of its own worth than the man she had met in the café.

*   ✱ ⛤ ✱

Tonight, I heard the sky crying and thought it was you. I know it is not. You are held. You are fed. You are sleeping, your breath small and brave. They told me I am not enough, and maybe I am not yet. But I am your father, and if there is any strength in me at all, I will spend it loving you.

*   ✱ ⛤ ✱

The words blurred. She pressed the paper to her chest, feeling the fragile fibers warm against her skin, the faint transfer of ink smudging onto her collarbone. Her breath came shallow, as if she had been running, though she had not moved at all. She had thought silence meant absence.

That if someone loved you, they would find a way to make noise. But here, in her hands, was one year of quiet that had never been empty at all. The room felt smaller suddenly, not because it was closing in, but because something long missing had finally arrived.

She reached for the following letter, hands trembling harder now. The one dated on her first birthday. The paper was thinner, almost translucent, where the ink had sunk too deep.

✻ ⚷ ✻

Happy first birthday, my little star. The cake sank in the middle, and the frosting looked like a rough sea. But I lit a candle anyway. If someday you like lemon, I will learn to bake it better. If you like chocolate, I will pretend it is not my favorite and give you a bigger slice. I am practicing a thousand small surrenders in case you need them.

✻ ⚷ ✻

Her lips parted in a sound between laughter and a sob. She could see it, the lopsided cake, the too-bright candle, the man sitting in a one-room apartment pretending it was a celebration. Her breath caught, sharp and sudden, and she pressed the letter flat against her chest until the ache steadied.

She began stacking the letters into small piles without meaning to. Some felt heavier than others. Some she set aside unopened, saving them for a strength she had not yet gathered. The shoe box remained open beside her, patient, as if it understood this was not something meant to be rushed.

✻ ⚷ ✻

The world feels heavier tonight. I am learning that missing you does not lessen, it changes shape. It becomes something you live inside of, like weather.

I saw a little girl with her father at the store today. She asked for lemon cookies. I bought a box even though I did not need it.

I ate one in the car and pretended we were sharing them. I will leave the rest here for you.

✳ ⇥ ✳

She wiped her face with her sleeve. The box beside her glowed faintly in the lamplight, its edges soft and worn. It did not look like cardboard anymore. It looked like a heartbeat. She reached for another letter, her tears still falling, her smile small but certain.

✳ ⇥ ✳

My little star, one began,

Today, I almost gave up. But then I remembered the sound of your laugh under the tree that day in the park, and the way the light settled on you that day. I will not give up. Not today. Not ever.

✳ ⇥ ✳

She closed her eyes, pressing the letter on her lips. It was not just the words, it was the trying in them, the refusal to stop loving her even when no one saw. The room around her blurred into a haze of lamplight and breath. Her pillow was damp; her hands stained faintly with old ink. She could feel something inside her rearranging, softening, like thaw after a long, brutal winter. At some point, exhaustion overtook her. The letters slid against her skin as she lay back, breath uneven, eyes aching.

She did not stop because she was finished. She stopped because her body could not hold any more without breaking. And for the first time in her life, Eleanor did not feel like she was trying to believe in love. She could feel it, warm, trembling, imperfect, but here. The letters rustled in her hands like leaves whispering to one another.

177

She lay back on the bed, the papers spread across her chest, the first box open beside her, and whispered to the ceiling, *"I hear you, Dad."* Then she closed her eyes and let herself weep, not for the years that had been stolen, but for the years that might still be given. Outside, the wind rose softly, turning the curtains like pages, carrying with it the faintest scent of rain. Night blurred into morning as she read, letter after letter, the soft crackle of paper becoming the heartbeat of the room. The lamp burned low, its light the color of honey poured through thin glass. Shadows shifted against her walls, climbing and falling like tides.

Each envelope carried its own weather. Some pages smelled faintly of smoke, as if they had survived nights near a single candle. Others carried the ghost of coffee and time, the faint oil from a hand that had held them too long before folding them shut. Somewhere in the night, she stopped noticing where one letter ended and the next began. She stopped trying to measure time at all. The dates blurred, not into years she had not yet seen, but into a single, continuous ache that refused to separate itself cleanly.

He repeated himself in his uneven script, circling the same feelings in different ways, as if meaning might hold if he said it often enough. Between them, his own words stitched through like thread: *I am learning that faith is sometimes smaller than breath. But even small breaths keep us alive.* There were letters about hunger and heat, about nights when he had no blanket but still lit a candle because rituals were a kind of warmth.

One described the winter so cold the ink had nearly frozen in the pen. Another told of bread left on his doorstep by a neighbor he had never met. *Kindness is just love wearing another name,* he had written.

There were letters of failure, missed chances, jobs lost, loneliness so vast it almost had its own gravity. Words that shook with confession and yet never begged for pity. Every one of them circled back to the same steady orbit, even here, even at the beginning: *You are not forgotten. You are loved.* The refrain repeated across the letters, changing only in tone, as if the words themselves were learning how to grow up beside her.

It was overwhelming. Like opening a window in a room, she had not realized it was suffocating. The air rushed in too fast, too much, too full of life. She gasped at first, then breathed deeper, slower, as if rediscovering how. Tears blurred the ink, making it shimmer. She pressed her sleeve to the page, but the salt only made the words more alive.

At some point, she began to read them aloud quietly, reverently, her voice bridging between then and now. Hearing them spoken filled the room with warmth that did not come from the lamp, but from something far older, something that had been waiting to be heard. When the letters began to blur together, she did not stop. Her eyes stung, her fingers were ink-stained, but still she turned page after page, as if stopping would mean losing him again.

Outside, dawn crept slowly into the world. The first light pressed through her blinds in thin, forgiving lines. It touched the papers scattered across her blanket, making the old ink glint faintly like veins of gold. Her voice faltered into silence. The pages rustled once, like a sigh. Eleanor lay back, exhaustion and peace mingling in her chest until she could not tell which was which. The letters fanned out across her blanket like wings.

She pressed one page beneath her cheek, the first letter, the one that had started it all.

The paper was soft from handling, warm now from her skin. Her eyes drifted shut, lashes wet, breath uneven. Even sleeping, her fingers clutched at the edges of the letters, as if afraid they would vanish if she let go. Somewhere beneath the drifting edge of sleep, a thought surfaced sharp enough to wake her: if her mother saw this box, she would take it. Or explain, calmly, why it was better not to keep it. She pictured that voice, gentle and final, the way it could turn an entire room into a locked door. Her fingers tightened around the paper, not from fear of ghosts, but from fear of losing something real.

Outside her window, the city stirred. Tires on wet streets, pigeons gathering on ledges, a siren wailing faintly somewhere far away. But in her room, the air was sacred, stilled, alive with words that had waited eighteen years to be read aloud. And as morning filled the space where night had kept vigil, she dreamed, not of loss, but of return. The letters shifted faintly in the breeze from the cracked window, whispering against one another, a rustle like breathing.

If words could hold a pulse, the room was full of it.

Morning light touched the scattered pages one by one, thin and forgiving. Eleanor sat up slowly, hair mussed, eyes swollen from tears that had dried mid-sleep. For a long time, she did not move.

She simply stared at the letters spread across her blanket, the written proof of a love that had lived quietly in the dark, waiting for her to find it. Then she began to gather them. One by one. Smoothing creases. Aligning corners. Managing each page as though it might tear if she rushed.

180

She folded them carefully back into the shoe box, the way one tucks a child back into bed after a long night of restlessness. When she finished, her hands paused above the box, unwilling to let the night end cleanly. She chose the first letter instead. The page that had crossed the distance before she ever knew there was something to cross.

She folded it carefully, not because it was fragile, but because it felt earned, and slipped it into her backpack, tucking it between her notebook and pencil pouch as if it belonged there. It was not the most hopeful letter. It was not the most polished. But it was the beginning. At school, the day moved on without waiting for her. Bells rang. Lockers slammed.

Teachers spoke over whiteboards streaked with yesterday's lessons. She moved through it all slightly out of step, as if her body were present but her center of gravity had shifted somewhere just behind her ribs. Between classes, she reached into her backpack more than once, not to read, just to feel the folded paper there. The quiet weight of it steadied her. It was not comfort exactly. It was orientation.

In history, when her teacher's voice blurred into a low hum, she found herself staring out the window at the flag snapping in the breeze, thinking not of dates or wars, but of time measured differently. In pages. In nights survived. In words written when no one was listening. At lunch, her friends laughed over something on a phone screen, the sound bright and distant. Eleanor smiled when she was meant to, nodded when prompted, but part of her attention stayed elsewhere. Not drifting. Anchored. She did not yet know all of what he had written.

She did not yet know how many years waited in boxes she had not seen. But she knew this much: someone had stayed awake for her. Someone had chosen her, quietly, again and again, without knowing if it would ever matter. For the first time she could remember, the world did not feel like something she had to chase in order to keep. It felt held. Not closed. Not finished. Just held.

And when she thought of seeing her father again, it was not anger that rose first. It was curiosity. Questions waiting for the right air. It was late afternoon at the park again, the same one where they had spoken before, but different now in the way light makes the familiar feel newly exposed. The trees wore the pale green of early spring, shy and tentative. A breeze stirred the fountain into silver ribbons, and the air smelled faintly of lilac and damp soil, as if the world itself were holding its breath.

Miles was already there, sitting on the same bench as before. His hands were folded, his shoulders pitched slightly forward, the posture of someone who had learned to brace for disappointment without meaning to. Another large paper bag sat beside him, untouched. Eleanor slowed as she approached. Her backpack rested heavier against her shoulders than it had that morning, not from weight, but from meaning.

He looked up when he sensed her, and though his mouth began to shape a greeting, he stopped himself. He only smiled. Careful. Earned. He nodded once toward the space beside him. She sat. For a while, they did not speak. The fountain filled the silence with its patient, tireless voice. Pigeons strutted across the path, cooing like gossipers, their shadows sharp against the pavement. She rested her hands in her lap, fingers threading together, then separating again.

She reached into her backpack and pulled out the single page she had kept. The first letter. The paper was softer now, its creases less severe, the ink faintly blurred where tears had touched it. She smoothed it against her knee, grounding herself in the feel of it. When she spoke, her voice was quiet, but steady. "You wrote about a bridge," she said. "In the first letter." Miles's breath caught. Not sharply. Almost imperceptibly.

He nodded once, slow. "Did you mean it?" She asked. "Or was it just… something you said because you didn't know what else to say?" He turned toward her fully then. His eyes searched her face, not for forgiveness, not for reassurance, but for permission to answer honestly. "I meant it," he said. His voice was rough, worn thin at the edges. "I didn't know if it would ever reach you. But I meant it." She looked down at the page again.

Her thumb traced the opening line, the familiar words anchoring her. "Why did you call me that?" She asked. Her voice wavered, just slightly. "My little star." For a moment, he didn't respond. His jaw tightened. His hands curled together, then loosened. "Because stars don't disappear," he said finally. "They just get harder to see when there's too much light in the way." He swallowed. "I needed to believe you were still there."
Something shifted between them. Not closure. Not absolution. But recognition. Eleanor folded the letter carefully, slower than she had before, as if the motion itself mattered. She placed it between them on the bench. "I didn't know if I should bring this," she said. "But it felt wrong not to." Miles stared at the page. His eyes shone, but he didn't reach for it. He only nodded. "I'm glad you did." They sat like that, the letter resting between them, the fountain murmuring on.

In his hands was another box. Not larger. Not smaller. Just the next. "Only if you want it," he said. No explanation. No framing. No attempt to guide what it might mean. Eleanor looked at it for a long moment before taking it. The weight was familiar now, but it did not feel the same. This one did not carry beginnings. *"Year Two,"* she read softly, her thumb tracing the edge where the cardboard had worn thin. He nodded once. She did not open it there.

That part, she was beginning to understand, belonged to her. A child laughed somewhere nearby, the sound bright and unguarded. She felt the air settle, not into silence, but into something steadier. Something alive. She didn't forgive him. Not yet. She didn't need to. But for the first time, the distance between them no longer felt unbridgeable. They sat until the light began to shift, until the edges of the trees turned amber and the afternoon leaned quietly toward evening.

And though the city moved around them, dogs tugging at leashes, buses sighing down the street, wind threading through branches, in that moment, it all felt briefly, reverently still.

As if the bridge had finally begun to take shape.

Over the next few weeks, he gave her more. Not all at once. Each one came the same way: wrapped in paper, edges softened by his handling, labeled in his careful, looping hand. **Year Three. Year Four. Year Five.** Sometimes he brought them to the café, sometimes to the park.

184

Once, he left one on the church steps with her name on it, as if some things were still too sacred to pass directly from hand to hand. Eleanor read them slowly. Not out of hesitation, but reverence. She read the way a starving person drinks: small, measured sips, afraid that too much too fast might undo her.

Some nights, she would light a candle the way she imagined he once had, the flicker trembling against the paper as if the flame itself recognized the words. Each page carried a different rhythm. **Year Three** was still uncertain, love written carefully, as if permanence might tempt disappointment.

✳ ☙ ✳

Your laugh is what I miss most, though maybe I have invented it. I imagine it sounds like bells dropped into water. I hold that sound close when the world feels too quiet

✳ ☙ ✳

Year Four carried steadiness. Small victories, routines beginning to hold.

✳ ☙ ✳

I am learning steadiness, one read at a time. *The kind that does not fade when no one is looking.*

✳ ☙ ✳

Year Five was heavier. The ink darker. The handwriting tighter. There were days when he sounded tired, lonely, older than his years. But even in the letters that shook with exhaustion, there was still the same promise that anchored them all: *You are not forgotten. You are loved.* Eleanor read until her eyes blurred. With every letter, the silence she had grown up inside began to lose its edge.

The walls of her mother's version of the story, *"He left. He did not care. He was not there,"* started to crack, not from anger, but from light leaking in.

185

It did not rewrite everything. It did not excuse
everything. But it revealed something truer: a man who had
failed and regretted it every day since; a man who had been
small, scared, and human, but who had loved her with a
devotion that outlived his mistakes. Some nights, she caught
herself talking back to the letters. Whispering answers into
the quiet. *"I got taller that year."* Or *"Yes, I do like lemon."*
Or *"I forgive you, but just for this page."* And somehow,
that felt enough for now. In her mother's house, silence
had always been a weapon, a way to end things, to close
doors, to win arguments without words. But here, in these
pages, silence became something else: a pause before
understanding. A place to rest.

The story was not perfect. It was not clean. But it was
alive. And for the first time, so was she.

It was another afternoon at the park, though she hadn't
planned it that way. The meeting had started as something
smaller; a walk, a return, a conversation she hadn't
rehearsed. But the air had shifted before she could stop
it. Miles stood near the fountain this time, not sitting. He
watched the water rise and fall as if it were keeping time
for him. When he saw her, relief crossed his face, followed
quickly by restraint. He waited.

Eleanor didn't sit right away. She reached into her bag
and pulled out a folded page. Not the first letter. Not the
bridge. This one was softer at the edges, handled more, the
paper remembering her touch. "There's something I need to
ask you," she said. His shoulders tightened, but he nodded.
"Okay."

She unfolded the letter slowly, though she knew the words by heart now. "You wrote about a balloon, Red," she said. He closed his eyes. She watched that small motion, the way it cost him something. "Did you really do that, or was it just… something you wrote because it sounded hopeful?" She asked. "I did it," he said. His voice was low, steady, unembellished. "I carried it for three blocks before I let it go." She swallowed. "Why?" He said. "Because I needed to believe there was still a way to send something to you, even if it came back empty." She looked down at the page again.

Her fingers traced the crease where the paper had once been folded small enough to fit inside a pocket. "I think I might have seen it," she said quietly. "Or maybe I wanted to." She shook her head once. "That's the part I don't know how to live with yet. Not whether you loved me. But why love didn't make you stay."

The words hung between them. Honest. Undecorated. Miles didn't rush to answer. When he spoke, it wasn't defense, it was accounting. "I thought staying away was the only way not to make things worse," he said. "I told myself I would come back when I had something solid to offer. A life that wouldn't collapse in your hands." He looked at her then. "I didn't understand that absence doesn't protect a child. It just teaches them how to live without you."

She felt the truth land, not gently, but accurately. "I'm trying to understand how to forgive you," she said. "Not because you're sorry. But because you tried. And because you never stopped." Her voice caught. "I don't know if trying is enough." He nodded. "I know." She folded the letter again, slower this time, and held it between them. "I don't want promises," she said. "I don't want explanations that make it easier." She met his eyes. "I want to know who you are now.

And whether you can stay present without needing to be redeemed." Miles breathed out. "I can do that," he said. "Even if it takes the rest of my life."

She didn't answer right away. The fountain murmured on. Wind lifted the edges of the trees. Finally, she said, "Then don't leave this time." He nodded once. "I won't." She sat beside him then, not touching, not closing the space entirely, but near enough to acknowledge it. The balloon did not rise between them.

But something steadier did.

★ ✪ ★

One evening, after reading a letter about the planetarium, how he had sat beneath the dome of stars and written her a story about constellations, Eleanor lay back on her bed, the page trembling lightly against her chest. He had written of Lyra, the harp, and Cygnus, the swan that never landed, and Aquila, the eagle that carried lightning for the gods.

He had ended the letter with a single, fragile line:

If I ever bring you light, I hope it is not to blind you, only to show you the way home.

✻ ⊶ ✻

The words glowed faintly in her mind long after she had turned off the lamp. The ceiling above her was a blank night sky, pale in the wash of moonlight spilling through her curtains. She closed her eyes. The hum of the city outside became an echo of something softer, the slow rhythm of passing cars, the whisper of wind through leaves, the faintest creak of the house settling.

All of it folding into a quiet she did not fear anymore. She imagined him years ago, sitting in that dark planetarium, head tilted back, surrounded by strangers, watching the artificial stars spark to life. Alone, but writing anyway. Believing that somehow, across the years and the miles, the story of those constellations might find her.

A warmth spread through her chest, subtle but certainly not the rush of joy, but something steadier, something that felt like gravity remembering what it is for. She exhaled slowly, her breath catching at the edge of a smile. Then, softly, into the dark, she whispered, *"Maybe love is real after all."*

The words felt strange on her tongue, not like a question this time, but like a truth rediscovered, something she had once known instinctively and had just now remembered how to believe. Outside her window, the clouds parted. A handful of stars blinked through, faint and scattered, but bright enough to be seen.

And for the first time in her life, she believed it. Not because the letters proved it. Not because he had stayed at this time. Because, for the first time, love no longer felt like a wound.

It felt like a language she could finally understand.

The Open Door

The final box sat heavier than the rest. Not because of weight, the paper inside was not thicker, the ink no darker, but because she had carried it differently. This one lived closer to her chest, as if her heart had learned to hold it long before her hands ever did. *Year Eighteen.* The words written on the lid were almost ghosted now, the ink faded to a soft gray, the cardboard soft where his fingers had once pressed it shut.

Eleanor traced the letters with her thumb, her breath catching as she felt the indentations, the small, uneven dips where his pen had pushed too hard. For a long time, she did not open it. She sat cross-legged on the floor, the box before her like an altar, the lamp behind her casting a halo of warm light that trembled on the walls. The window was cracked open, and the sound of wind brushing through the trees outside carried the faint smell of rain, the kind of air that always came before changing.

When she finally lifted the lid, her pulse stuttered. The scent that rose was faint, but familiar: old paper, coffee, the ghost of candle wax. There were fewer letters this time, but they were thicker somehow, the handwriting steadier, slower, a man writing not from youth or guilt, but from clarity.

Each word measured, each sentence deliberate, as though he knew these pages might be the last bridge between them. She unfolded the first. The ink was clean, patient. The tone had changed. The earlier letters had been filled with longing and apology; these carried something quieter, more grounded. The ache was still there, but now it was laced with peace.

My little star,
I have learned that love is not what survives time. Love is what time survives.

Eleanor closed her eyes, her breath trembling out. She could almost hear his voice when she read now. She did not have to imagine the younger man at the table, lonely and unsure. She saw *him*, the man she had met, older, worn but luminous in a way that comes only from carrying sorrow and still choosing tenderness.

She read the next page.

It is strange, writing now that I know you are almost grown. I used to think I was waiting for you to find me. I was really waiting for myself to become someone worth seeing. I hope I am, or at least close. I wish I had learned how to stay, even when I am afraid.

Her throat tightened. The lamp hummed softly. Outside, the rain had started with small drops at first, then steady, tapping against the glass in an even rhythm. She reached for the following letter, but it trembled in her hands. Her vision blurred. She pressed her sleeve to her face, wiped, then unfolded it anyway, refusing to stop now.

This one was dated only a week before her eighteenth birthday. The paper was clean, unmarried. His handwriting was small but sure, each letter clear and deliberate, as if every curve of the pen were a prayer.

My little star,
If you wish, the door is open. Not wide. Not bright. But open. Always open.

If you never walk through, I will still sit on the other side until my last breath, waiting with the light on. But if you do… I will finally be whole.

✶ ⚷ ✶

The last word smudged slightly, as though his hand had trembled, or a tear had fallen before the ink could dry. Eleanor's own hands shook now. Her breath broke in uneven bursts. Tears slid down her cheeks before she realized she was crying, hot, unrestrained, relentless. She clutched the page to her chest and bent forward, her forehead against her knees, the letter pressed between her heart and her ribs.

Her sobs came in waves, years of silence breaking open all at once. The rain fell harder. She thought of him sitting alone at his table, writing this one final letter. She imagined the candle burning low, the window fogged with his breath, the sound of his pen scratching hope into paper. She pictured him whispering her name under his breath as he folded the page, sealing it with a trembling kind of faith. And now here she was, holding it.

Holding him. It was unbearable and holy. When she finally lifted her head, her face was streaked with tears, her hair damp with sweat and grief. The words illuminated by a single, flickering lamp. Her eyes caught on the final sentence, *waiting with the light on.* She turned toward the window.

The rain had eased, and through the watery glass she could see the faint gleam of a streetlamp outside, steady, golden, unwavering. It looked, impossibly, like a signal. She rose, slowly, clutching the letter in both hands. Her legs trembled beneath her.

She did not know what she would say, what would happen, or how the next moment might look, but she knew what she needed to do. The words still echoed in her chest: *If you wish, the door is open.* She did not have to decide if she forgave him. She did not have to name what she was feeling. All she had to do was walk. So, she did.

She pulled on her coat, tucked the letter safely against her heart, and stepped out into the wet night, the air cool, the pavement shining with reflected light, the scent of rain like something alive. And as she made her way through the quiet streets, moving toward whatever came next, her pulse steady with every step, the thought came to her like a whisper, carried by the wind: *He kept the light on.*

And this time, she was walking toward it.

A few days later, she found him again. Not at the bench. Not where things had already been said. On the bridge just beyond it. The air carried that soft hush of late afternoon, when the world holds its breath between day and dusk. He rose the instant he saw her. Hope flickered across his face so naked, so unguarded, that it nearly undid her. Every wrinkle, every hollow, every tremor in his hands spoke of the years between them, the waiting, the writing, the wanting.

She did not sit across from him this time. She sat beside him. For a moment, neither spoke. The fountain murmured behind them, coins glinting in the shallow water like the remnants of other people's wishes. "I read them," she said finally. Her voice shook, but she did not hide it. "All of them." He drew in a breath so sharp it sounded like a gasp. His fingers tightened on the edge of the bench.

"And?" He asked, the single word small, frightened, braced for both mercy and destruction. "They hurt," she admitted, her voice breaking on the word. "Because they showed me what I missed. Every birthday. Every moment. All those nights you wrote instead of being here." She paused, breathing through the ache. "But they healed, too. Because they showed me, I was not forgotten. Not once. Not ever."

He bowed his head. His shoulders trembled. "I never wanted you to feel forgotten," he said hoarsely. "That's been my prayer every night, that somehow, even across all that silence, you'd know." Eleanor turned toward him then, really turned. The light caught in her hair, gold at the edges, and her eyes were wet but steady. "I don't know how to do this," she said softly.

"I do not know how to be a daughter to someone I have only just met. I do not know how to stop waiting for everything to disappear." He met her gaze, his own eyes rimmed red, and for once did not try to fill the silence. He just let it breathe between them with the ache, the uncertainty, the miracle of being seen at last. "You don't have to know," he whispered finally. *"We'll learn together."* She exhaled, the sound half laugh, half sob. "Together," she repeated, as if evaluating the word for weight. He nodded, the motion trembling but sure. "One letter at a time," he said.

The fountain sprayed a fine mist that settled cool against their skin. Somewhere, a child's laughter rang out, clear and bright, the kind of sound that used to hurt but now only reminded them what hope could feel like when it returned. Eleanor looked down at her hands, then at his. After a long hesitation, she reached across the space between them and took his hand. It was warm. Solid. Human.

For a moment, neither spoke. The silence was not a
wound anymore. It was a promise, fragile, but real. Above
them, the first streetlamp flickered on, casting a soft gold
light over their joined hands. And for the first time, the
world did not feel like it was holding its breath. It felt like
it had just begun to exhale. A breeze stirred the fountain's
spray, carrying the faint smell of wet stone and new grass.

The air shimmered with that clean, just-washed light that
comes after rain, the kind that makes everything, benches,
pigeons, even strangers' faces, look briefly forgiven. The
sun broke free of the clouds and laid a path of gold across
the water. It was not dramatic, just certain, like a truth too
gentle to announce itself.

The droplets caught the light and scattered it in a
thousand trembling directions, so that for a moment, the
world seemed to breathe in color. She reached into her bag.
Her fingers brushed the worn spine of a book, the cool
metal of the star necklace, and finally the folded red balloon
letter, the one she carried everywhere now. Its edges had
softened from handling, corners bending inward as if the
paper itself had learned the shape of her grip.

She drew it out carefully, the red still faintly visible
along the creases, the ink gone to sepia in places. He
recognized it at once, though he had not seen it since the
day he had let it rise over the river all those years ago. It
was as though time had carried it in invisible hands and
placed it back here, between them. For a long moment,
she said nothing. Neither did he. The water behind them
whispered its constant song, the city moving on at its edges,
with distant sirens, a child's laugh, the low hum of traffic.
The world was continuing, as it always had.

Eleanor held the letter between them, the thin paper trembling slightly in the breeze. Her hand was steady, but her eyes were not. "It's yours," she said finally, her voice low, unsure. "Or maybe it's ours." He looked at it, at her, at the sunlight resting on her shoulder. And in that quiet, he understood that the letter was no longer a message or a relic; *it was a bridge.* A thread connecting the years of silence to the breath of now. He did not reach for it. He did not need to.

The act of her holding it out was the answer to every prayer he had never dared to speak aloud. Between them, the paper fluttered once, catching the light like a heartbeat. And the fountain went on singing its unending song, the water crossing itself in endless circles beginning, ending, starting again. "This one," she said.

"This is the one I will keep forever. Because it reminds me you were looking for me, even when I did not know to look back." His tears slipped free then, falling fast. He pressed a hand over his face, shaking with the force of it. Eleanor touched his arm, tentative, trembling, and felt him steady beneath her palm. "I'm not saying it's easy," she whispered. "I am not saying I forgive everything. But... I am here. And I want to try."

He lowered his hand, eyes shining. "That is all I ever dreamed of. Just the chance to try." They sat there for a long time, not speaking. The silence between them was different now, not sharp, not hollow. It had shape, warmth, and breath. It was no longer something that divided them, but something that could be shared, like a bench or a sky. The fountain murmured behind them, its rhythm steady and low. A breeze stirred the water, sending tiny ripples across its surface until the reflection of the sky broke apart and reassembled again, just as they were doing now.

Eleanor leaned back slightly, her shoulders brushing his. For the first time, the contact did not make her flinch. It steadied her. "You know," she said at last, her voice soft but sure, "I've drawn a thousand doors in my notebooks." He turned toward her, a small, tired smile spreading through the tears that still clung to his lashes. "I've written a thousand letters," he said quietly. "Maybe they were always meant to meet."

She let out a shaky laugh, the kind that comes from relief more than amusement. "Then maybe this," she said, "is what the doorway looks like when it finally opens." For a moment, the air held still around them, as if the park itself were listening. She reached into her pocket and pulled out the star-shaped necklace, the silver charm dulled slightly from years of being thumbed and held. She turned it over in her palm, letting the late light glint across its edges. "Then let's call this the first key," she whispered. The words hung between them, delicate and certain. He hesitated, his breath catching, old instincts urging him to move slowly, to ask permission, to make sure she would not disappear if he reached too far.

Then, gently, he extended his hand. She looked at it for a heartbeat, at the lines, the tremor, the proof of work and waiting, and then she placed her hand in his. Their fingers found each other awkwardly at first, then more surely. Clumsy, but real. Neither of them spoke. They did not need to. The fountain shimmered in the fading light, scattering gold across the surface.

A single maple leaf drifted down, landing beside their reflection, then spinning slowly in the current until it was carried away. He gave her hand a slight squeeze, tentative, reverent, and she did not pull away.

For the first time, neither of them was reaching across the absence. They were holding on to presence.

And above them, as the first stars began to appear in the deepening blue, it felt as if the sky itself was unlocking.

For eighteen years, the story had been silent and absent. Now, it is imperfect, fragile, alive. The air around them felt different, charged with a quiet electricity that only truth could make. The sky above Sierra Mesa had begun to shift toward evening, that dusky blue hour where everything softens, the light, the edges, even the heart. They strolled along the park path, side by side. Not touching at first. Just close enough that their shadows overlapped on the pavement.

She could feel his breath beside her, steady, uneven, real. It felt strange and miraculous at once, to walk next to someone she had once only known through paper and ink. He was the first to break the silence. "You look like your mother," he said carefully, as if testing whether it was safe to say her name into the open air. Eleanor's mouth curved faintly. "People say that" she murmured. "But I think I smile like you."

He turned to her, startled, not by the words themselves, but by the gentleness in them. "You… think that?" She nodded. "I did not use to know what that smile meant. I thought it was something careless in me, something too much. But it was just.." She hesitated, searching for it, "something waiting to belong to someone."

His throat tightened. "Then I hope I'm worthy of it," he said softly. "I've wanted to be, for a long time."

They paused beneath the old oak near the fountain. Its branches arched overhead like a cathedral ceiling. The air smelled faintly of rain and earth and the cinnamon rolls from a nearby cart. She tilted her head back, watching the first star flicker into view. "Do you still write?" She asked. He smiled faintly. "Sometimes. Not as much as I used to. I ran out of words that hurt." She glanced at him, her eyes luminous in the fading light. "Maybe you were just waiting for the right story to start again."

"You sound like someone who knows what she's talking about." Miles chuckled the kind of laugh that came from somewhere deep, unused for too long. "I've had a lot of practice with unfinished stories," she said, her tone teasing but her eyes damp. "This one... feels different." He looked at her then, really looked. The small scar near her eyebrow, the way she shifted her weight when she was nervous, the steadiness in her gaze that had not been there when they first met at the café. "Different good?" He asked.

"Different real," she said. The sound of the fountain filled the silence that followed, steady and alive. He reached into his pocket and pulled out something wrapped in tissue, worn at the edges from being managed too often. "I meant to give you this earlier," he said quietly. "It's not much." She unwrapped it carefully. Inside was the pale-yellow ribbon, the one he had taken from her drawer all those years ago. It was frayed now, soft as breath, the color faded almost ivory.

"I kept it," he said. "Every job, every move, every winter. It was all I had of you that felt alive. I thought... it should go back where it belongs." Eleanor's lip trembled. She touched the ribbon as if it might dissolve under her fingers. "It already belonged to you," she whispered.

He swallowed hard. "It belonged to both of us. It was waiting for this." She nodded, tears spilling freely now. "You waited eighteen years," she said, her voice breaking. "I'd have waited a lifetime," he said. "But I'm glad I don't have to." The sun dipped fully below the horizon, and the park lights flickered on one by one, hailing them in soft gold. She tucked the ribbon into her palm beside the star necklace.

"Then maybe," she said, voice trembling but specific, "we should stop calling it waiting." Miles smiled, that tired, luminous smile she recognized from the letters. "What should we call it, then?" She met his gaze, steady now. "Living," she said. He laughed quietly, choked, undone, and she joined him, and for a moment, their laughter tangled with the hum of the fountain and the sigh of the wind, turning the park into something holy. As they began to walk again, their hands brushed. Neither of them pulled away.

The stars thickened overhead, spilling silver through the branches. Eleanor thought of all the doors she had drawn, all the keys she had carried, all the questions she had whispered into the dark. Tonight, for the first time, she had an answer. The door was not just open. She had stepped through.

And on the other hand, someone was waiting with the light still on.

Not behind her. Not ahead of her.

With her.

First Key

The building was smaller than Eleanor expected. Not imposing. Not cinematic. Just a low, pale structure with wide windows and a flag that snapped lightly in the wind, the sound sharp and ordinary. The kind of place people walked into every day without ceremony and walked out changed anyway. She checked the address twice before going in. Inside, the air smelled faintly of toner and disinfectant. Shoes scuffed against tile.

Somewhere down the hall, a phone rang and rang before stopping. A woman laughed quietly behind a counter, then lowered her voice again. Life continuing. Eleanor stood just inside the door, her backpack resting against her spine, the weight familiar now. Not heavy. Anchoring. A sign pointed toward **Advising & Financial Aid.** She followed it. The waiting room was half full. Plastic chairs. A low table stacked with pamphlets she did not touch. *Transfer Pathways. First-Generation Student Support. Deadlines Matter.*

She read the titles without picking them up, the words settling in her chest like coordinates instead of promises. When her name was called, it took her a second to realize it. She rose and followed the counselor into a small office with a desk pushed too close to the wall and a framed poster listing scholarship criteria in tidy bullet points.

The woman introduced herself, shook Eleanor's hand, and gestured toward the chair across from her. "Let's take a look at where you are," she said, already pulling up a screen. They spoke in facts. Credits completed. Credits pending. GPA. Residency status. Income thresholds. The counselor did not soften her language or offer reassurance. She did not need to.

She answered clearly, asked questions when she had them, and wrote notes on the margin of a folded sheet of paper she had brought with her. When the counselor slid the scholarship forms across the desk, she did not hesitate. She read each line carefully. Initialed where required. Signed her name once. Then again. The pen felt solid in her hand. "This one has a response essay," the counselor said, tapping the page. "Short. Two hundred words. We're looking for clarity more than narrative."

Eleanor nodded. "I can do that." The counselor smiled, small but approving. "Most people overthink it." She did not say anything. She did not feel the need to explain that she had spent eighteen years learning how to speak plainly about what mattered. When the meeting ended, she stepped back into the hallway and paused, just long enough to fold the papers carefully and slide them into her backpack. Not crumpled. Not hidden. Exactly where they belonged.

Outside, the sun had shifted. The light fell different now, sharper, less forgiving. She walked across the quad without stopping, past students sitting on the grass, past a bulletin board layered with flyers for clubs and protests and lost keys. She did not look back. That evening, she sat at her desk with the window open and the papers spread neatly in front of her. The sounds of the neighborhood drifted in: a car door closing, someone calling a name, wind threading through leaves.

She wrote the essay in one sitting. Not because it was easy. Because it was honest. When she finished, she read it once, corrected a sentence, and saved the file without rereading it again. She closed her laptop and leaned back in her chair, the motion unremarkable, final. The next morning, she dropped the forms in the mail slot on her way out. She did not watch them fall.

That afternoon, she met Miles at the park. He was already there, sitting on the bench with his hands folded loosely, his posture less guarded than it had been weeks ago. When he saw her, he stood, then stopped himself, smiling instead. "You're early," he said. "So are you," she smiled. They sat side by side, the fountain murmuring behind them. Eleanor reached into her bag and pulled out a single sheet of paper. Not a letter. Not something fragile.

Just a form, folded cleanly. "I went today," she said. He did not ask where. He waited. "I'm applying," she continued. "Community college first. Transfer after." He nodded, "That sounds right," the movement steady. "I'm not asking for help," she added. "I just wanted you to know." He answered quickly, "I know, and I'm proud of you." The words landed without weight. Without pressure. She accepted them the way she had learned to accept truth: quietly.

They sat for a while longer, watching the light shift across the water. When she stood to leave, she did not feel like she was stepping away from anything. She felt oriented. Forward-facing. Balanced. As she walked home, the city moved around her, indifferent and alive.

And for the first time, it felt exactly right.

Epilogue ~ Light in the Window

One year later, the house smelled of bread. Not the kind that comes from a bakery, precise and polished, but the kind that rises unevenly in a chipped pan with dough that has been touched too much, kneaded by hands still learning the rhythm of patience. The air was warm with it, buttery and alive, the scent curling down the narrow hallway and settling in the curtains like sunlight that refused to leave.

It was not much of a house, just a rented two-bedroom on a quiet street where maples dropped their golden leaves across the walk in autumn, carpeting the steps in color before winter came to claim them. But it was theirs now. A place that no longer belonged only to memory or longing. The walls carried their laughter the way walls do when they have learned the shape of a family. The floor creaked in familiar spots. The windows stuck sometimes when it rained, but the light found its way anyway.

Eleanor sat at the small kitchen table, the one he had sanded down years ago when it still bore someone else's fork marks. Now it bore theirs: faint pencil lines from her homework, a crescent from his coffee cup, crumbs from the midnight toast they made when the world felt too large to sleep through. She turned the pages of her navy notebook; the same one she had once filled with doors.

The paper had grown heavier with time, swollen slightly from spilled tea and the weight of living. The doors were still there, hundreds of them, but they looked different now. Less like barriers. More like invitations. On one of the newer pages, she had drawn a house, this house, with a crooked chimney, a leaning fence, and light spilling from every window. Beneath it she had written, in her careful, looping script: *Not perfect. But ours.*

He came in from the garden, brushing dirt from his hands, his face flushed from the chill. "It's rising," he said, nodding toward the oven, as if that were newsworthy of celebration. Eleanor smiled. "It's working," she answered. He poured two mugs of coffee and set one beside her notebook. Steam rose between them, soft and silver in the afternoon light. From the stove came the faint pop and hiss of the oven settling. "They're almost done," he said. "The rolls, the ones I learned from that TikTok video years ago."

She laughed. "The ones that fell like bricks the first time?" He grinned, "Yeah. These ones might be more brick than roll, too," as he rubbed the back of his neck. "Doesn't matter," she said, closing her notebook gently. "They smell like home." He leaned against the counter, pretending to study the timer, but just watching her, the way she blew across the top of her coffee before drinking, the way she tucked her hair behind her ear when she was thinking.

Outside, the wind moved through the maple branches, scattering a few late leaves across the porch. The smell of the rolls filled the house, sweet, buttery, imperfect, the scent of something finally, quietly right. For a moment, neither spoke. The silence was not absent anymore. It was comfort. The quiet hum of a life rebuilt, the kind of stillness that lives only where love has learned to stay. They drifted down like slow applause from the world itself.

She looked down at her drawing, then up at him, and whispered, to herself, *"We found the light."* He smiled that small, tired, beautiful smile that comes from people who have earned their peace one breath at a time. He reached across the table, resting his hand on hers, a simple touch, nothing grand, nothing cinematic. Just steady. The kind of touch that says: *I am here. You are here. That is enough.*

And in that small, ordinary moment, every year of
waiting folded itself into peace. From the stove, he pulled
out the rolls then a loaf of bread, grinning sheepishly at
the uneven crust. The scent filled the room, warm, yeasty,
home. "Still not as good as Texas Roadhouse," he said,
setting it down. Eleanor laughed softly. "Doesn't have
to be." He sliced into it with a careful hand, steam rising
between them like a blessing. The crust flaked unevenly, the
inside soft and perfect in its imperfection.

He passed her the first piece. "You like lemon, right?"
He asked, teasing. She rolled her eyes, "You remembered."
Smiling as she tore off a piece and blew gently on the
steam. "I remember everything," he said quietly, not as
confession but as gratitude. They ate in silence, the kind
that does not need to fill itself. The kind that feels like
grace. Outside, the last of the daylight slipped through the
branches, pooling gold across the table. The air smelled of
bread and beginnings.

And somewhere between the warmth of the oven and
the pulse of their joined hands, the years stopped mattering.
Only the moment remained, whole, fragile, and infinite.
"It's better," she said, slicing into it as steam rose. "Because
you made it." He laughed softly, rubbing the back of his
neck. Even after a year, some moments still startled him,
the casual way she said I love you, the ease with which she
sat in a chair he had once only imagined full.

Their life together was not flawless. It was never meant
to be. Some mornings began with light pouring through
the kitchen window, the smell of coffee and butter, and
something like peace. Other mornings began with distance,
the kind that does not shout but settles quietly in the air,
heavy and invisible, waiting to be named. The silence came
back sometimes.

It carried old wounds, dragging the ghosts of years when the only sound between them had been absence itself. There were nights when she would retreat behind her bedroom door, and he would sit in the living room, elbows on his knees, hearing every second tick past like penance. There were mornings when words came out sharper than either of them meant, when fear dressed itself as anger and left them both bleeding in the same house from the same wound.

But now, the silence was shared, not imposed. Now it had edges they could trace together. Now the anger had a place to land, not a void to vanish into, but a table, a conversation, a hand extended after the storm. Forgiveness was not quick, but it was real. They were learning the hard truth that love, if it is to last, must be repaired more often than it is celebrated.

They learned slowly from each other, in fragments: He learned she loved lemon tea more than coffee, that she made it strong with honey instead of sugar, and that she drank it with her legs tucked under her on the couch, the mug balanced carefully on one knee. Eleanor learned he hummed under his breath while washing dishes, not songs she recognized, just fragments of melody, wordless and full of thought. Sometimes she would stop in the doorway and listen, knowing it was not really a tune; it was memory trying to stay gentle.

He learned she hated storms but loved their smell, the charged sweetness before the first drop hit, the way the world held its breath just before it broke. When thunder came, she flinched. When lightning flashed, she counted softly under her breath to ground herself. He never told her he did the same. Eleanor learned he still lit a candle on her birthday, even though she was here to blow it out herself. He called it a habit, but she knew better.

To him, ritual was a language, a way to keep meaning alive. That small flame had stood in for her all those years, and even now, he could not let it go. Each discovery was a letter written in the present, no longer sealed in a shoe box or folded between guilt and hope.

These were letters that breathed, that spoke through small acts: a cup of tea left waiting, a hand steadied on a shoulder, a quiet laugh shared in a kitchen that once knew only echoes. There were still days when the past came knocking, a memory, a question, a wound reopening for no good reason. But there was always someone to answer the door.

And sometimes, that was enough to save them both.

On the night of her twentieth birthday, the world seemed softer than usual, as if it, too, remembered. They stood together on the porch as the neighborhood glowed gold, with squares of lamplight in other people's windows and fragments of lives unfolding in quiet rooms. The air was cool, carrying the faint scent of lilac and wood smoke. Somewhere down the street, someone laughed; somewhere else, a dog barked once, then stopped.

Eleanor held the star necklace in her palm, its metal edges worn smooth by years of worry and touch. It caught the light from the porch and flickered once, as if it still remembered its purpose, a small piece of sky meant to be held. He struck a match and lit a single candle, setting it carefully on the porch railing between them. The tiny flame leaned toward her, steady in the breeze. "Shouldn't there be cake?" She teased, her voice gentle, teasing, yet shy.

"There is," he said, smiling. "But the candle goes first. Always." She looked at him, really looked, and saw all the years folded into his face: the late nights, the letters, the weight he had carried and learned to set down. In that moment, he was neither the man who had waited nor the man who had lost. He was just her father, standing beside her under a sky full of familiar names.

She leaned closer, their shoulders brushing. The contact was simple, yet something inside both steadied at once. Together, they whispered, *"Happy birthday, my little star,"* before she drew a breath and blew out the candle. The flame surrendered easily, its brief life ending in a curl of smoke that twisted upward like a gray ribbon vanishing into the dark.

For years, that darkness had frightened them both. But now it felt different. Now it felt like space. The smoke thinned, caught by the wind, and disappeared. But its warmth lingered between them, an invisible thread trying to breathe. Neither of them feared the dark anymore. They stood a moment longer, watching the horizon bruise into deep blue as stars began to puncture through. Somewhere above them, Vega was rising.

He pointed once, quietly. Eleanor nodded. No words were needed. Inside, the house glowed with warm light spilling from every window, just as she had once drawn it, with a crooked roof, a leaning fence, and light where there had been shadow. For the first time, the story did not feel like a door closing. Instead, it felt like a homecoming.

The story did not end. It arrived.

If this story meant something to you, the most powerful way to support it is by leaving a quick review.

Leave a Review on Amazon

It only takes a minute and helps other readers discover the book.

**Can't review on Amazon?
You can also rate or review on Goodreads.**

Thank you for reading and supporting us.

**Henry Daniel Archunde Jr.
True North Writings**